D1521368

The Swedish Bakery:
A feminine ode

A novel by

Mona Lisa Moru

The Swedish Bakery:
A feminine ode

MONA LISA MORU

For information: 1223 Wilshire Blvd Los Angeles, CA 90017
Moru, Mona Lisa
The Swedish Bakery: A Feminine Ode
ISBN: 9798586408808

Chapters

This book is a homage to all bakeries in Uppsala where I grew up on endless Fika. Locations where my awareness of time and place have dampened, and where my mind and imagination have swirled above and beyond.

Dwelling

The scent of yeast rising is her most cherished part of the morning. The smell of life expanding. The first time she tried braiding challah was when she was twenty years old, and Marie had felt clumsy, disoriented, and hugely disappointed.

"This is way too complicated for me," she thought before throwing the dough in the trash.

Back then Marie had planned to save up some money from her job at the grocery store, travel the world, and maybe do some yoga and learn meditation. Little did Marie know that her grandmother (with whom she didn't have much of a relationship) was to become ill, die, and leave her 'The Swedish Bakery'.

With a depressed mother and an alcoholic sister, it was pretty clear which one of them was suited to take over.

At the time she thought, "I'll work at the bakery for a while, and then sell it to pay for my travels".

A while turned into forty years, and today Marie has got a feel for the dough.

Marie's dreams were put on hold, and her meditation became seeing metaphors in the bakery every day, feeling as though life communicates with her through the baking process.

The braiding process is a dear one for Marie, it helps her feel on track. Nothing gives her such a sense of accomplishment as creating beautiful braided challah. She could give a damn about anything else.

Marie taught herself how to make a nice even strand from the dough by doing it over and over again. It became easier after she let go of the idea that she was going to travel the world. Letting go helps Marie stay in the moment, and when she accepts her destiny, life flows more effortlessly.

All the braids are made from strands, so Marie has learned impeccably how to make a foundational strand shape. In order to do that, Marie made peace with the fact that she is probably going to stay at the bakery in Stockholm for the rest of her days. This acceptance was hard in the beginning, especially in her mid-twenties, the late twenties, early thirties, and late thirties —after that it was easier, and letting go of her dreams became effortless.

"It's just not meant to be."

Instead of traveling, Marie has her ritual of watching Swedish television during the quiet hours at the bakery, sneaking to the back counter like a bandit to watch some of her most desired movies:

Astrid Lindgren's "Pippi Longstocking", "Karlsson on the Roof", and "Rasmus and the Tramp". A guilty pleasure she feels no guilt about.

These movies give Marie adventures she'll never experience; characters she'll most likely never encounter, and playfulness to feed her inner child that she couldn't get elsewhere. This ritual is intimate and personal for her.

Astrid Lindgren has been Marie's most adored author since childhood, and she likes to throw herself into the sphere of these characters, pretending it is her world, swimming in another microcosm, if only for an instant, a twinkling. Until of course a customer asks for a pastry or refill and she has to press pause, which disturbs her reverie.

Marie divides the dough into the number of strands that she'll need, making sure each portion is equal in volume, like someone would when braiding hair. She divides the dough into three equal portions.

The three portions remind Marie of her own family; each portion representing one family member. Marie, her mother Brigit, and her twin sister Cilla (her actual name is Cecilia, but she doesn't like to be called that so to avoid one of her emotional breakdowns they all keep to her nickname, Cilla).

Her twin Cilla has since nursery been an extremely self-centered person. It all started with the fire and pretty much hasn't changed since. Marie was burnt as well, has visible burn marks on both hands and left chin, but not to the degree that her twin has scars. Cilla resents her to this day and out of her anger has left Marie to take care of their mother Birgit, alone.

Birgit is slipping into dementia, and although Marie loves her mother, she would love a helping hand from Cilla. Becoming a drunk is egotistical, and Marie has never thought of alcoholism in any other way, so she's done feeling guilt-ridden and apologetic for her sister.

Marie takes one of the dough portions and rolls it out with a rolling pin until it is flat and about a quarter-inch thick, using strength and pressure from both hands. She pulls the dough towards her, thinking how she has tried to get closer to Cilla for decades —but Cilla is too busy being irresponsible and carrying around hatred. Birgit has desperately, dramatically beseeched Marie to stay in touch with her twin, because as a mother she can't bear the thought of her Cilla being upset. Birgit is a guilty parent and a genius at parenting poorly from such emotions.

Even pressure is kept on the dough as Marie rolls it to prevent air pockets from collecting in the strand. Just like Marie rolls the dough back and forth with her two hands, she has kept those same two hands active with work at the bakery and care for her mother. She never grumbles much. Who would care about her protests?

By angling her hands Marie creates a beautiful shape outward, then applies gentle pressure to taper the dough on the outer edges. The bakery bell rings. It's not Elsa.

"Where is she?" she thinks to herself.

She impatiently rolls the dough to taper the other end of the strand, waiting for Elsa is making Marie go frantic and the dough is paying the price.

Marie checks her Instagram account —no comments on the bakery's latest post: a picture of the new painting that she'd just hung in the bakery by her most admired artist, Carl Larsson, an oil painting titled 'Midvinterblot 1915' (Midwinter sacrifice). She loves how radical it is, and the fact it was at one time called 'Sweden's most controversial painting'. The painting portrays a Swedish king at the Temple of Uppsala who was sacrificed to avert famine. It was shunned by museums for its controversial subject matter for a very long time.

Marie has a great fondness for Larsson's art, and keeps two more of his paintings hanging above the biggest table in the middle of the bakery, on the brick wall across from each other: 'Breakfast in the open 1913', and 'Breakfast under the Big Birch 1895'.

Larsson's art awakens marvelous emotions within Marie. His winsome paintings throw Marie right into the late nineteenth and early twentieth centuries, to homes with delightful and elegant environments in the Swedish countryside. With an impeccable taste for patterns and colors, Marie feels as if she is living with the characters in the paintings; having breakfast with them under the birch trees, mostly women and children. Every time Marie looks at his paintings she feels like a giddy child who gets to stay up late for Midsummer night's eve. It works every time and she smiles to herself fascinated by her own imagination. Her fantasy heaves her into the painting, leaning against the big birch tree in 'Breakfast in the Open' across from the woman in a white linen dress, listening to the sound of the violin playing and the amusement and cackles coming from the big table with the folks massed around it for a picnic.

Thinking of Elsa

F ive years ago Marie hired Elsa as a part-time worker for the bakery when Elsa was only twenty-two years old and was taking drama classes from a private acting coach.

There had been an instant spark and flare between them; they both felt as if they had known each other eternally. Elsa used to also read about Pippi with her mother every night before going to sleep. That was one of Elsa's most vivid and meaningful memories of her mother, along with the flames —her mother Edith died in a car crash with seven-year-old Elsa in the backseat.

Edith Beijer was one of the most prominent and celebrated actresses in the history of Swedish cinema. Elsa has never known the particulars of what took control of her mother that day when she was only seven years old, nor has she ever googled anything to try and fathom why Edith did what she did.

Knowing your own mother had committed suicide by crashing her car with you in the backseat, and knowing the public is aware of that fact, is enough enlightenment. No need to dive into the specifics.

Marie has for the longest time urged Elsa to plunge into Edith's past, to absolve her, and release her own heartache.

"I think it would be healing for you, Elsa."

"The woman who bore me as a child tried to execute me, there's nothing healing about that."

"There is more to the story little swan, I promise you."

"I don't want to know anything about it," she'd say as she turned away arrogantly.

Marie knows that Elsa is auditioning this morning —an audition that may or may not help her get accepted into one of Sweden's most prestigious drama schools.

Two hours have gone by and Marie is still awaiting Elsa to return, hopefully with news of prosperity.

"I have been accepted!" these are the words Marie so hopes to hear.

She is waiting for the dough and making sure it has completely risen, because if not the strands may expand while braiding.

Marie's intuition tells her Elsa has been colossal today, but she doesn't want to assume anything in advance (although she does). She pulls up her phone, checks Instagram, still no comments about the new painting she posted and only thirteen likes.

"Should I start braiding?" she debates with herself... She yearns to take Elsa off her mind, knowing that she will have to continue braiding until it is fully finished. If Marie walks away from the half-braided challah she might lose her place in the braid, which can make the process a lot more problematic. She decides to start braiding.

Making even strands into beautiful braids took practice, although Marie always knew it would come naturally since she learned how to braid her own hair as a little girl. Braiding her hair has taught Marie to be very aware of the middle strand —keeping an eye on the middle strand keeps her unafraid of much, and certain of all.

Memoir

Elsa walks across the middle of the street in tears without glancing around. She is graceful, neat, and dishy, in an uncommon way. Everyone sees and appreciates her particular charm and individuality, except her. With old earbuds in, (she didn't care for the new wireless ones) Elsa hears nothing but her favorite artist, Ted Gardestad, and his lyrics for "Come Give Me Love".

Ted Gardestad was a Swedish singer mostly active in the seventies and eighties until his death by suicide in 1997. Elsa has always been fascinated by his choice of how he left this world — throwing himself in front of a train. Why would he do that on the day of Midsummer when life seemed to be going so well for him?

For inspirational reasons, she listens to his combined boogie-woogie and country music when she is feeling down. Maybe he felt inadequate, just like she has felt for as long as she can remember.

She's especially embarrassed by the fact she is Edith Beijer's daughter.

"The daughter from the backseat of the car," as some like to call her.

The fact that people recognize her at the bakery some days does not help. Every time she hears someone say her mom's name, Elsa feels bad. She still hasn't figured out if she feels dreadful for her own sake, or for her mom. Probably both.

"I feel ashamed and flustered about the fact I can't live up to her name."

She said this in tears to Marie as they were closing the bakery one night.

"Then don't try to live up to her name," Marie said with a barbaric tone.

"I am sorry Elsa, but you have to stop trying to be something or someone you're not. You'll wake up one day realizing you've thrown your life away wearing a mask. Die wearing a mask. Don't you want to go to your grave as you? Do you want to die as another person?"

Elsa thought about Marie and her pitiful Instagram account, the account that no one cares about but Marie.

Elsa hates social media, it is heartbreaking to her that it has come close to ruining a whole generation. In her opinion, Instagram is an illusion, she doesn't think it has anything to do with reality and feels sorrow for people that are on it.

"It gives people a chance to live in another reality, an existence that is solely in the mind, and create a version of themselves that does not exist in real life."

She has a hard time understanding the authenticity of it. If there's anything that aggravates Elsa when it comes to Marie, it's the fact that she is so active on social platforms as an entity, a kind of persona that is not in sync with Marie's real day to day life. She is regularly posting pictures of her gaudy candles, lavish paintings, frilly pastries, nostalgic movies, and her bohemian flower child spiritual quotes —What about the dying of her mother and the drinking of her sister? There is nothing on there that displays even a glimpse of how Marie really looks, works, or lives, nor is there anything flashing how alone she feels on the inside, under the surface, behind all the facade. Other than that, she couldn't have yearned for a better ally or associate (Elsa owns a piece of the bakery after helping Marie out in a financial crisis), or friend. Who is wearing a mask really? Both of them, but Ted's singing voice is soothing and consoling anyway.

At the bakery, Marie sets the loaf on a baking sheet and puts it in the oven, attends the bread, and awaits Elsa.

She spruces up after two guests who have just had chamomile tea before their quick departure.

When people just visit the bakery they are Marie's guests, and if they buy something from her, customers, which of course she prefers.

Marie always appreciates a worthy listening session to the developing conversations that are going on at the bakery, her favored part being filling Elsa in on the latest buzz. Elsa doesn't enjoy the babble quite as much as Marie, who thinks it's great slander for free.

"You don't have to enroll, but you still get entertained." Marie always declares like a toddler anticipating Santa Claus on Christmas Eve.

It's in Elsa's nature to push and serve people, rather than chattering and mocking people behind their backs. She has many times indicated to Marie that this side of her behavior is contradictory and conflicts with her stated beliefs.

"How can you post nifty spiritual-quotes, when you are constantly slandering and making fun of people?"

Elsa has a hard time being sympathetic with how the two go together, as she's always accepted some level of spirituality herself; although she doesn't have any strict interpretations on what means who, and who meant what. There is something deeper and more profound than what the eye can see. She can't justify it, but she can feel it —she trusts, respects, and observes the mystery of it. Elsa has never felt the need to post on social media her impressions or conclusions, thinking it cheapens her as a human being and gives her away as a person. The things Elsa enjoys the most are the things she swallows and keeps to herself. That way the things she keeps remain sweet to her; no one else can drag them in the mud, have viewpoints on them, or try to make her assumptions and emotions smaller in any way. Elsa relishes keeping this kind of separation in all her relationships, not by shutting people off, but by having some discretion and keeping some prudence.

The customers at the bakery will often come to Elsa for consultation and input, as she is up to date with what's going on in their lives anyway. She is a genius at giving verbal prescriptions but has yet to achieve applying any of them to her own life, often thinking:

"Wow, what I just expressed to that person (often to Judy, the Flower shop owner) is some exceptional shit, why don't I live by that myself?"

It leaves Elsa feeling crummy and lousy about herself and the poor choices she keeps making.

It irritates Elsa additionally that she has told Judy to leave her husband who is flippant and uncivil with her —at the same time, Elsa is living with Simon (the struggling musician who's been nicknamed Voldemort) who has lived off of her for nearly two years.

Simon is lazy, cheeky, out of job, ungracious, and talks down to Elsa every chance he gets —yet she stays. Knowing this about him, seeing these things clearly, she still stays.

Elsa thinks of her dad often in relation to Simon. Was her dad a marvelous man?

Elsa's mom never spoke about him, or maybe she did and Elsa is just struggling to remember?

In her defense, Elsa was only seven years old at the time her mom attempted to assassinate her.

Perhaps her dad was a marvelous man, but an atrocious father? Or a marvelous father but an evil man?

"I wonder how he treats women?" she asked Marie at a certain point. Is he delicate? Delightful? Refreshing? Or does he bore them to death?

Elsa tried to look her father up a few years ago without any thought of gain or profit. She googled 'Edith Beijer boyfriend', then stopped herself instantly. It felt too close to home, and other shit started coming up too. It was clear that Edith never spoke about her boyfriends in the press, having lived a very secluded and private life, apart from her work.

Elsa once heard a rumor that her father wasn't even Swedish, but Italian or French or something like that. All Elsa has left after her mother's death is Edith's jewelry, clothes, makeup, money, and some micro-fame in Stockholm she does nothing with — except for trying to be an actress herself.

To use the fact she had a famous mother to become an "influencer" was out of the question, even though Marie encouraged it.

"Post some makeup, make money, and you'll get cast in movies."

One thing Elsa knew about Edith was that she had great undeniable talent, something she would never try to fake. Ted continues to croon, "Come Give Me Love".

The door to the bakery opens, Marie looks up from behind the counter. It's Elsa, finally. Marie is concerned, understanding by the look on Elsa's face that the audition turned to absolute shit.

Elsa walks to the backroom, throws her backpack onto the floor, and continues out into the kitchen with Marie following. Elsa sits down on the floor hugging her knees.

"It's okay if you don't make it this time, little swan. No matter what, you tried your best."

Elsa's throat hurts. It's that feeling, the feeling of having held back tears for years. Those clumps in your throat that want to be felt and listened to. Elsa finally releases, knowing with Marie it is safe, and it feels good. Thank god she never wears makeup.

Through tears, she tells Marie about the whole auditioning experience, that as soon as she walked into the auditioning room the lady had recognized her last name. 'Beijer' —of course.

"You're not Edith Beijer's daughter, are you?" she squawked like an aggravating crow with a raspy, thick and cracked, five packs of cigarettes a day voice.

The crow lady's comment had immediately reminded Elsa of how horrid and useless she feels about herself. Worst of all was that the flames of the car crash came suddenly into the room as if there and alive, flickering in her face.

Elsa recalls Edith's face in the back mirror, Marilyn Monroe like smoking a cigarette with the window open on that Swedish summer night, makeup in disarray and crying.

"Why are you crying, mom?"

The memory after the image of her mom crying is the flames, and then the funeral.

Seven-year-old Elsa could not apprehend why so many people tried to talk and take pictures of her. Seven-year-old Elsa couldn't fathom why she had to go stay with foster parents and their creepy son. Seven-year-old Elsa could not grasp why she had to fear the nights alone with her foster brother who crept around her bedroom. She wished for her loudmouth mom to come in and save her. Free her. Why hadn't she? Did Edith want Elsa to get hurt? Had Elsa not listened to her mom, and was now being punished? Elsa started feeling like she had done something terribly wrong, and that feeling never really left her. Year by year, she kept suppressing her thoughts until they were no longer active in the mind. It hadn't been until her late teens when the thoughts had become strong and loud that she experienced violent episodes of rage —but still, she refused to listen, leaving her in emotional disarray. In error.

There she was, auditioning, mumbling, trembling, feeling nauseous, scared, and again —inadequate. That horrible feeling that is so familiar, the most natural feeling in the world. Her whole life Elsa felt inadequate and incomplete, not knowing what was missing.

Elsa tries to go back to the memories from her sessions with Eva from time to time; the therapist from boarding school, the only person who knew the truth about the ' horrible nights' at the foster home. Life took over and she stopped making time for sessions with Eva.

Eva has known Elsa since she was twelve years old; from the age she was sent to boarding school and stopped enduring the ' horrible nights'. In some ways, it is still painful to think about Eva who reminds her of all her misfortune and suffering. But what Elsa hasn't come to terms with, is that the suffering will not go away until she faces it head-on.

Elsa tells Marie how she stormed out.

"I ran out like a dingbat."

Marie listens, thinking that the drama school based in Stockholm might not be the place for Elsa, but does not tell her so. Marie has never liked folks telling other folks what to do with their lives, strongly believing that life is all about self-discovery.

"Make mistakes, learn from them, and get over yourself," she always says.

Marie does not want to be harsh on Elsa. The last thing she wants to do is to model the behavior of a destructive parent.

Parents who think they know what is best for their children, filling their heads with nonsense and absurdity until there is only gibberish echoing in there —resulting in the children not knowing who they are, or what they want from life.

Mothers who make their daughters feel guilty about every single step they take, judging their every move.

Mothers letting their children behave narcissistically with no consequences, all stemming from the guilt of the mother, resulting in the child growing up to think all their wrongdoings are justified: What Birgit did to Cilla —how Cilla treats her sister Marie.

Marie usually sets a timer while baking but today she kept herself too busy, so both Marie and Elsa smelled the burnt bread.

"Did you forget to set the timer, Marie?"

Elsa gets up and takes the burning loaf out of the oven. Marie runs for water.

"Heavens, I got too distracted." Marie pours water onto the loaf, leaving it black like Swedish salt licorice. Smoke rises. Elsa looks at the loaf. It looks like bread after-life, deceased and dead-beat dead.

"Could this day get any more daunting and depressing?" says Elsa while Marie tries hard to cover up her laughter. Elsa sees it and is not at all bothered by it.

"Do you ever feel... I don't know Marie, but do you ever feel meaningless?"

The answer is yes, but Marie knows that Elsa has a lot to let out, so whenever she begins to speak, Marie lets her do so, hoping she will understand that talking about your feelings is actually communicating with yourself.

"I can't explain how I feel, I feel like a good person overall, a good friend, a loyal girlfriend, but at the same time I feel like the biggest piece of shit ever. How can those emotions go on in my body at the same time? And how can they both speak to me so strongly?"

Elsa rubs her face, wiping off salty tears.

"A good person, the biggest piece of shit, a good person and a piece of shit," she repeats, comparing the two.

"How come, Marie?" Marie grabs a chair, sits down next to her face to face.

"Duality darling. Us humans, we are complex beings, we carry both the light and the dark." Elsa looks at her pessimistically.

"And how can I get rid of the dark?" she asks, hoping for an instant solution that will make her feel whole and complete.

"You can't get rid of the dark within you, the more you try to, the stronger it gets. Both the light and the dark will always be present in us Elsa, it's all about which one you give weight to. We decide whether to dwell on positive or negative thoughts."

Elsa listens. She loves this part of Marie, the part that is sensible and wise, telling Elsa things she's never heard before.

"I could go on forever with my darkness, complain about my sister and cry about being the only one that is taking care of our mother. Cry about the fact that my mother always took Cilla's side when we were growing up, even though she was a very mean person who created a lot of damage and sadness in everyone around her."

Elsa looks at Marie with deep admiration, knowing what burdens she carries, knowing that Marie has had to stay in the bakery for way longer than she had originally planned. Innocently, with no harsh intent, Elsa's biggest nightmare is to become like Marie. She is desperate to become something or someone. She is scared of getting stuck in the bakery like Marie. It is a very comfortable and familiar place, and those places can sometimes be the traps in life.

"I don't want to criticize Cilla anymore, I don't want to carry anger and disappointment any longer, and it keeps me from feeling the joys and all the bliss in life. I don't want to become an old grouchy hag."

For the first time today, Elsa smiles, and it means the world to Marie that she's been able to put that smile on her face. Watching Elsa suffer is worse than waxing her mustache off. Marie would take Elsa's pain away if she had the power to do so; she'd take the pain instead of Elsa if she could. But it is not possible to take someone else's pain away, the person in pain has to make that decision for themselves, and Marie knows this very well from her own experience.

Elsa sits back up from the floor.

"Thank you for being my friend Marie, there is absolutely nothing I wouldn't do for you."

It's obvious that their love for each other goes both ways, secretly they feel like mother and daughter.

They have never spoken of it because they don't have to. It is boisterous and clear, but in the silences rather than in the words they share. Somewhere on a bridge spanning their emotions, desire and affection, they have become just that. Mother and Daughter.

Meilleur Ami

For Marie, the delight of making tea is in the ritual. The more she repeats the series of steps for brewing tea, the more she finds satisfaction.

The more Elsa and Amira go through in their friendship, the more they enjoy and appreciate that friendship.

"It's all about the details when it comes to making a perfect cup of tea," says Marie while boiling water.

Elsa and Marie finish up closing the bakery. At the end of every Friday, they stay there longer to wait for Amira, Elsa's best friend since they were eighteen. They've been best friends for seven years now after meeting at a children's summer camp that they were both working at.

"Of course you can just boil some water and grab a tea bag, but if you want to elevate the experience, there are a couple of extra steps you can take."

Elsa smiles at Marie, looking out the window and expecting Amira any minute.

Marie warms the water in the teapot, as always starting with cold water and steeping whole leaf tea. She sets the timer so the tea is steeped for the right amount of time.

Marie starts thinking about time, about Amira and Elsa —like the leaves of the tea, the two young women are different, but also so alike.

Amira, born and raised in Sweden, brought up by a strict and controlling immigrant mother from Syria and an absent Swedish father; and Elsa, brought up by many different people, in various homes. Amira is studying to become a journalist so she can do what she loves the most: writing.

While studying she is working part-time at a kindergarten to get by. Her greatest passion is a blog about women's rights.

Elsa is working at the bakery because it's easy and comfortable while trying to become an actress.

Amira wears a hijab, Elsa wears jeans and t-shirts.

Amira hates Elsa's boyfriend Voldemort and exudes a steely persona —but at the core, Amira is a very insecure and sensitive person. That sensitivity the two of them have in common, and that's really where their friendship resides. Amira does not conform herself to typical modest Arab standards, especially when it comes to her fashion. She wears her headscarves always showing some hair in the front or on the sides. She likes to blend modesty with elegance and wit. She wears hijabs in many colors and different styles, satisfying her creative side. Many people have judged her for not wearing the hijab 'the right way' but that doesn't stop her from being a genius at harmonizing fabrics together. She will never go for a bright colored outfit if she's wearing a vivid scarf, or go for a sharp headscarf when wearing a rich and flashy outfit.

Her hijabs are often homemade, colorful, and printed with various patterns. When it's cold outside, they transform into shawls topped with neon-colored beanies.

Elsa had been overjoyed when she met Amira at the summer camp. Amira wasn't selfish (like the girls from the boarding school), nor did she care about the fact of whose daughter Elsa was, and didn't even know of Edith Beijer, had never heard of her, which was so refreshing to Elsa. Amira was the opposite of a burden and had completely different interests, she loves Fleetwood Mac, Joan Didion, Simone De Beauvoir, and contemporary art. She could give a fuck about the film industry.

What Elsa doesn't know about her friendship with Amira is that she is the driving force behind Amira's bravery. Amira would not be so daring in her writing if it wasn't for Elsa's warm love and enduring support. Every time Amira is insecure about an article she's written, Elsa is there to give her constructive criticism and notes. Every time Amira is scared of being 'too much', or having too radical an opinion on her blog, Elsa is there to tell her to press send with determination.

Elsa constantly makes sure that Amira posts her articles, even when it sometimes frightens Amira that she doesn't know what people will think of her viewpoints.

Although Amira's blog hasn't grown or found its readers after five years of her working on it, Elsa refuses to let Amira retire from writing it.

If a week goes by without a new article, Elsa is there to nudge Amira to keep writing. Amira will have excuses, none of them ever good enough for Elsa to tolerate. She'll indulge in a sentence or two, but the goal is always to push Amira back to the keyboard.

"I don't feel any enthusiasm right now. There's no inspiration at the moment."

"A professional writer will write nevertheless."

"But it's just not flowing right now."

"Well, sit down and just start, that way it'll come to you."

She never lets Amira get away with her whys and wherefores. No excuses.

People always say that there are no excuses, but the problem is in reality —that there are too many excuses.

Amira finally arrives and sits down with her laptop. She's in low spirits, tries to act happy, but Elsa knows her way too well, and can tell that Amira isn't as enthusiastic and rowdy as usual, the only thing ecstatic is her bright yellow jumper —matching with her light lavender shawl and a pair of big round silver earrings.

Marie sits down and fills three cups of tea as soon as she sees Amira —over steeping tea leads to a bitter cup, and there is nothing worse than a cup of bitter tea in Marie's opinion.

Amira tells Elsa that her boss from the kindergarten doesn't think that wearing a hijab the way she does is very fitting and that some of the children's parents are grumbling over Amira's 'choice of outfits'.

"Choice of outfits? That's the most brainless comment I've heard in my life!"

Elsa is in a fury, she hates it when people attack Amira and is sick of culture being so obsessed with people's appearances. She loves how daring and unusual Amira's clothes are.

"Someone keeps posting negative comments on my blog, calling out my hijab, mocking my heritage, and even making fun of my nose."

Amira has heard comments about her 'pointy' nose her whole life, even her family makes fun of it. She has always been the kind of woman to focus on other things when something is trying to creep up and make her feel bad about herself, whether it be thoughts, family, or blog comments. The nose comments are particularly hurtful and something she's struggled to get over for a long time.

"I've been blogging for almost five years now! Nobody cares about what I'm trying to put out there. It hasn't even grown one percent! In fact, I am getting fewer clicks."

Marie chimes in with one of her attempts at a metaphor:

"I never leave the tea leaves sitting in water since that just makes the tea too strong and bitter."

Elsa and Amira swap a look, letting each other know they're on the same page. The two young women know Marie too well to let that comment slip between the cracks. They know she loves to give her teachings in indirect ways that are sometimes opaque but have learned how to interpret them.

"Are you saying I shouldn't think of the negative comments posted on my blog for too long or I'll become bitter?" Amira chirps.

Elsa laughs, knowing that's exactly what Marie means.

Marie uses the tea filter to take the leaves out after the first steeping, then ads them back in after she refills the teapot with water.

"I think your blog is the most intellectual ever, Amira." Elsa offers.

Elsa means what she says, she's never read anything like it. No one is more brutally honest, raw, and well-educated than Amira. Her writing is brilliant and very academic. She reminds you to take a deep look at yourself and the words you use that in an ignorant way can hurt other people. The cruel expressions aimed towards certain cultures or religions, and those that stick you into a category that is the most misunderstood and degraded in society —Womanhood.

Elsa believes that the harsh comments are coming from people that are too scared of looking within, even if just for a momentary glimpse. Amira's writing forces you to review yourself whether you like it or not.

"I just want people to understand me, not be so judgmental, and..."

Marie interrupts,

"Why is it so important for other people to understand you?"

Marie goes on to tell them that people will only listen from their own level of perception and that you can't really change anyone's understanding. It's hopeless.

"So she should just give up? Just stop writing then?"

Elsa does not agree with Marie at all, she thinks that having a blog helps to raise awareness, teach people, and to change bloodthirsty minds. She is proud of Amira.

Marie explains "I don't mean that you should let up on your writing or halt anything in any way. I meant to refrain from trying to make people understand, stop forcing it. The best way to make people understand who you are is actually to just live it."

"I suppose."

"Write for your own sake instead of writing for anyone else. That's where the art is, within you, for you, and if someone else relates, then that's glorious."

Delicately sipping on hot tea, Marie conscientiously continues to utter her platitudes softly, not wanting to agitate either one of them.

Elsa whispers to Amira,

"Then why doesn't she stop posting annoying pictures to try to get likes?"

Thankfully Marie doesn't hear this, too fixated on what she's going to say next.

"Imagine if the whole world just turned within instead of running around on the streets." Marie stops herself, thinking she's being too aloof, but then changes her mind and continues.

"If every single person turned within to look at themselves rather than looking at everything outside of them, then the world would be a better joint, believe me."

"How are people not turning within?" asks a curious Amira.

"People wear the mask of self-righteousness, wear the mask of 'I am fighting for a cause', wear the mask of blaming everything on the outside, wear the mask of being a victim, wear the mask of always being busy with something, saving the world, avoiding, distractions —all of these masks so that they don't have to face the truth of what's really going on within themselves." says a proud Marie.

"Those are some masks." At this point, Amira doesn't take anything personally considering that Marie's ideas are more about herself and what she has come to in life.

"Judging the world is a way of escaping yourself, your true self. Escaping what's really going on with you." Marie continues.

Elsa thinks that is exactly what Marie is doing by being on social media, avoiding herself, and dodging the real problems. Elsa is still fascinated by seeing someone give advice about something that really applies to themselves. Elsa wonders if it's conscious or unconscious behavior on Marie's part?

"Why do people do that, why do people judge and flee themselves like that?" Elsa wonders, trying to get Marie to see that she is talking to her about her.

Marie knows exactly why, but doesn't really say anything, she knows why people flee because she does it too. Marie judges politics, the world, organizations, people around her, just so she can avoid herself and her emotions. Her true feelings are eerie, and it is sometimes more painless to focus on something else rather than dwelling deep into her own fecal matter.

Unfortunately for Elsa, Marie isn't thinking out loud this time. She continues to wonder if Marie's stream of words are conscious or unconscious.

Later that evening, Elsa arrives back home from the bakery, Simon is playing video games (instead of writing music and trying to get it out there) as usual. He has been cranky since the moment Elsa got home, mostly nagging about chores that have not been done to his liking, along with a billion other things.

Simon has a chillingly high-pitched, somewhat hair-raising voice, and what is scary about that is —the fact he never yells but still—, his voice can be the spookiest most spine-chilling in the world. Hence, Voldemort.

Elsa opens up her laptop and searches for Amira's blog, at the end of the most recent post she clicks on the comments button and types:

"I myself wear a hijab and I want to thank you for being a strong voice for us, you have helped me tremendously."

Amira sees the comment, not believing that someone has found inspiration in her latest blog post. She beams so wide her cheeks hurt, feeling refueled and happy. What she doesn't know is that Elsa does this often, she'll comment with different names to even out the opposing comments on Amira's blog. It makes Elsa feel good. There is nothing like being kind to someone without telling the person about it. It is the real act of giving and Elsa doesn't want anything in return, except Amira's contentment.

But she can't help but wonder,

"Am I doing this because I am selfish? Or Am I really doing this for Amira?"

The act of giving is sometimes hard for Elsa to understand, she is commenting on the posts for Amira's happiness, yes, but she also feels good about doing it, so is she doing it for herself to feel good, or for Amira to feel good?

Elsa is so anxious that even when contributing positivity she feels she's being hoggish.

Both Amira and Elsa put their laptops away and although separate, leave each other with emotions of euphoria. It's as if Voldemort's weird intimidating voice was made silent in Elsa's life for all of eternity, and the gloomy negative comments on Amira's blog, all of them, shrunk into nonexistence. Suddenly maleficence was overturned by friendship because true friendship triumphs over all —anyone and everything.

PMS and A Partisan

Stockholm is dark and freezing. There is nothing worse than cold Sweden along with bad news. Elsa was rejected from drama school.

February is the darkest time of the year when you barely see daylight. It's dark when you get up in the morning, and darkening again when you finish work. People's appearances and moods match the weather —everyone walks around like shadows with misty eyes between heavy fog. Each person's soul is dim and dusk with attitudes as murky as the darkest sorcerer's demeanor. You're lucky if you get a smile from one person between the months of October to April. But most likely, you won't be lucky.

To try and inspirit the unhappy and winter-ripped residents of Stockholm, the bakery focuses on gooey and rich chocolate cakes.

This week it is Elsa's turn to bake and she is alone at the bakery before opening —five am— The bakery opens at seven. This is her darling hour before the surge begins. Elsa has lit up the fireplace and prepared some of the ingredients she'll need for baking, then sits down in front of the fireplace in a red armchair with golden metal legs. She tries to soothe her anxiety caused by PMS by sipping a cup of chamomile tea slowly. Elsa looks around, appreciating the silence. The silent hours are when she can hear her own thoughts; acknowledge and enjoy how much she loves this bakery. It is so adorable, neat, and can barely hold the occupancy of twenty-five people, which Elsa finds pleasant. She loves how personal and intimate the bakery is. How beautifully the metal chairs match with the wooden tables, and how fancy Marie's colorful paintings look matching with the lavish mustard yellow cushions thrown around between chairs. Elsa's favored area is the brick wall behind the fireplace. The other walls are made out of wood and she appreciates how a mismatch can actually become a match.

Gerda, the good-looking but aging fashion queen who always slightly smells of alcohol (definitely comes from money judging from her extravagant sense of style) walks past the bakery in a big white fur coat. She sometimes visits the bakery and Elsa likes it when she does —she thinks Gerda is coldish but in a refreshing and mysterious way.

It won't be long until Elsa will start hearing students chatter as they are buying their morning black coffee, weeping about the train delays and cancellations because of 'weather disruptions'. This often happens with the trains between Stockholm and Uppsala.

Judy, the woman from the flower shop across the street will come in with her destroyed and dispirited winter personality asking for a green tea she won't pay for. Others will come in to sit down and suck on each other's low-spirited downer stories until their brains bleed. They'll enter with their frozen frost feet and pessimistic sense of selfhood, all stemming from seasonal depression —and it's not even mid-February yet. People start to find the state of having an individual identity again in March, thinking 'April will come soon', until it snows again, which melts the next day —turns into slush— and lets down a whole nation of stillborn optimism and daydreaming.

Elsa will be left behind having listened to all this behind the counter, while in her mind she goes over the details of one of the worst dinners she's ever had, never mind that it's also a greasy slick hair day.

Simon and Amira had started bickering while having dinner at Elsa's place. On top of that unpleasant memory banging around in her head she is going to menstruate in nine days, meaning she was at the height of her PMS with an uneasy feeling in the ovaries. The suicidal thoughts have been milder this month believe it or not, but the emotional swings are really bad. Elsa feels tremendous sadness, apathy, and experiences episodes of rage straight from hell. She thinks back to when she was fifteen and menstruating, living at the boarding school, and taking ballet classes. She wasn't allowed to wear panties, so she tried a tampon without having the slightest idea of how it works and bled through to her skirt, resulting in sobbing in the girl's bathroom. When you missed three classes in ballet, you were no longer allowed to dance in performances. That incident was her third time missing ballet class, so she was kicked out of the final performance. It seems to Elsa that women get punished for bleeding, and feels society looks at tampons and feminine hygiene stuff as a luxury rather than necessity. Not understanding why women have to pay for tampons or pads, neither can she understand why these items are taxed by men.

Elsa has described her PMS to Marie:

"Like a car speeding the fastest it can, then right before crashing into a stone wall, it slams on the breaks."

Elsa's emotions go crazy right up until she feels she is about to die, and then finally, she bleeds. But the car ride is long, jarred, uneven, choppy, and very bumpy.

Marie had told Elsa over the phone to take it easy at the bakery this morning, she said it didn't matter if she got to bake the cake or not. Marie heard Elsa's story about the fight between Amira and Simon and felt bad that Elsa had been put in the middle.

Amira will be stopping by any minute to talk things out. Elsa feels uptight and nervous, knowing she's done something terribly wrong by not standing up more for her friend. With tender breasts, an achy headache, and creamy sticky vaginal discharge landing in her pantyliners, she takes her birth control pill before heading over to the kitchen to start baking. Going through an abortion helps to remind you to not skip a dose.

Elsa puts an apron on and follows the recipe, the one she has memorized. She's already preheated the oven to three hundred degrees and lightly greased an eight-inch pie plate.

Blending flour, cocoa powder, and salt, Elsa can't understand why it's so hard to mix relationships with friendships. She sets the first ingredients aside, then stirs eggs into the sugar until smooth. Making it work between a best friend and boyfriend has so far resulted in catastrophe at every attempt. They can never all hang out without some kind of fiasco going down. Simon doesn't get along with Amira; and Amira, straight up, can't stand Simon (or the non-existing music that he claims to be working on). Elsa adds the flour to the mixture, stirring until combined. The anxiety is intense this morning, she feels like she can't breathe but tries to tell her mind it's not true.

"You're okay Elsa, you can breathe, and your body is just playing tricks on you. Don't take it so seriously."

Simon, being the prick he is, was of course acting like the prick he is at the dinner. This time, with Amira over visiting at their apartment. The three of them were eating when Elsa poured Simon some more wine.

"How many times have I told you, that's not the way to hold a wine bottle?"

Elsa backed down immediately, she didn't want to get into an altercation in front of Amira. Lately, she'd been backing down all the time to avoid battles. But they've reached a point in their relationship where there is no backing down as an alternative, Simon wants to get into fights all the time, probably because he feels junky about himself, and projecting his shit onto Elsa makes him feel better —not in the long run but for the few moments of a clash, it works. Simon isn't as whimsical as he used to be back when they had just met three years ago. He still hasn't gotten a job, which he promised he would two and a half years ago! He doesn't appreciate anything Elsa does for him anymore, not that he really ever did.

Frankly, she can no longer bear the thought of Simon touching her. It still happens, not because she wants it to but rather to avoid getting into combat followed by cross-examination.

Elsa speculates all the time whether she should be with him any longer.

"Why do we know, but act like we don't?" she writes on a post-it note with a black marker pen. She crumbles and tosses it away on the bedroom floor.

Amira had gotten very annoyed with Simon when the wine bottle incident happened and had for the first time spoken up on Elsa's behalf:

"Have you been serving at a five-star restaurant lately or something? What makes you think you know anything about pouring wine?"

Simon looked at her with instant loathing, proving what Amira has always said about him.

"Voldemort hates me."

"Stop calling him that," Elsa muttered not wanting a scene.

According to Simon, Amira is too rowdy and intrusive, but what she really is, is curious and analytical.

"She's my girlfriend, don't interfere, okay?"

"So what she's your girlfriend? It doesn't mean you own her."

Amira looks at Elsa, disappointed she isn't being defended, even more, disappointed to see how beaten Elsa really is in this relationship. Just for the fact she won't stand up for herself.

"She needs to learn," Simon says.

Elsa knew that as soon as Amira left she'd be up for some emotional terror and wasn't looking forward to it.

"I want to learn. I think it's good you try to teach me things."

Amira studies Elsa with great disappointment, not believing who her best friend has become.

Is Elsa really this defeated? To the point where she can't tell someone to just lay off for a second? What a setback, what a blow.

Amira grabbed her bag and aimed for the door.

"Wait."

Elsa followed, but it was too late. She was gone. Back at the table, the spooky voice awaited.

"Why didn't you defend me?"

"Because I hate your guts and can't even stand looking at you anymore, you son of a tart." she thought but, of course, kept to herself.

"Why aren't we doing what we should be doing?"

Elsa wrote once again on a post-it note that got crumbled and tossed somewhere on her bedroom floor, preparing for Simon's intimidation that was going to begin once he was done brushing his teeth.

"Why didn't you defend me?"

Elsa will never hear the end of it.

"You never stand up for me, you are showing a lack in our relationship."

Simon would then go on an attack on Amira, always blaming the clash on the fact that Amira is 'miserable'.

That is always his argument for why Amira does what she does, including her blog. In his mind, Amira is an unhappy woman who is out of her mind jealous of her best friend's relationship because her own family won't let her date.

Elsa knew part of that was true, but only the part about Amira's strict mother. Elsa has never liked the fact that people judge Amira by the way she dresses. Just because Amira has a certain faith, it doesn't mean she has all the restrictions people assume comes with being a Muslim.

Amira is free to make her own decisions, especially since her younger sister Sara got married. After that happy event, the pressure got taken off of her a bit.

*

Elsa adds in the vanilla extract and butter, stirs until well combined, and pours it all into a greased pie plate.

Amira walks into the bakery wearing a long green coat and a red beanie over her black hijab. Elsa as always appreciates how Amira blends clothes with intensity and unexpected undertones.

Amira looks tired, they haven't spoken in four days, since the wine bottle incident. Elsa had texted her but had gotten no response. Amira takes off her coat, brushes off the snow from her beanie, and sits down in one of the armchairs by the fireplace.

"I'll be right out, just let me throw this in the oven," Elsa yells from the kitchen.

Elsa places the pan on the lower rack of the preheated oven and sets the timer for thirty-five minutes. She takes her apron off and goes to sit down in the facing armchair by the fireplace. The particular mood is as cold as the frost on the bakery windows from the outside.

Amira can feel that it's strange between them and in an attempt to break the ice she hands Elsa some roasted almond nuts she just picked up from the winter market in Gamla Stan (old town) on her way here.

"Where's the chocolate?" asks Elsa.

"It's not good to eat sugar while Pmsing, it makes your symptoms worse."

Elsa thinks it's pretty cute that Amira tracks her cycle. That's how in tune they are —they know when the other is in the PMS dimension, about to bleed. For Elsa, the PMS dimension is like being on another planet (she called it her Pussflow), completely alone with her darkness and cynical thoughts.

"Thank you," Elsa says while eating a couple of roasted almonds.

"No worries, I passed by the winter market on my way here."

"How was it?"

"Romantic but cold."

"Thank you for fighting for me the other night, I'm really aware of how foolish I behaved."

Elsa feels good about the fact someone else is seeing that there is something freaky about Simon. And that it's not her fault, at least not all her fault. It feels good to see someone stand up against him, to see someone challenge him. Maybe now Simon will come to terms with the fact he is behaving kooky. Perhaps he'll change now? Wishful thinking.

"You are welcome, I guess," says Amira without looking at her.

Elsa feels appalled about not standing up to Simon that evening, wishing she had more bravery in this situation and in all other situations.

"I should have said something when he went off on you. I really should have."

Amira doesn't agree, at least not anymore. She can finally understand the situation from Elsa's point of view. The past few days have made Amira realize that Elsa is stuck in an emotionally abusive relationship and that it's not as easy to get out of as people think.

How can she ask Elsa to defend her when she is not even able to do that for herself? Amira realizes that this is what true friendship is about, or should be —to see situations beyond yourself and your own emotions. To be there and support Elsa, instead of thinking about her own pain and opinions about the situation, because the one in real torment is Elsa and not herself. Amira decides she is going to let this one slip, hoping Elsa will wake up and wish death upon Voldemort (Amira's thoughts can get very intense and bitter when she doesn't like someone). She chooses to accept that Elsa is in an abused state of mind, so she won't take anything personally. It's about a poisonous relationship, and Amira doesn't know how to handle it anymore —she does know she will be there for Elsa, giving her love and support as long as her friend wants and needs it. Amira thinks this, not realizing how noxious this relationship will start to feel for her to be around.

Elsa needs to reach her own limit when it comes to her relationship with Voldemort. Amira can't do it for her. Nobody else can. All Amira can do for Elsa right now is to be there as a friend and not judge her, which is tough.

"I am not mad at you Elsa, you don't owe me anything," Amira says after an awkward silence.

"Of course I do."

"You owe yourself something, and that is to figure out why you are letting someone treat you as poorly as he does."

Amira's words hurt like a punch to the kidney. Elsa is trying to endure the conversation without crying, but it's hard.

"Find that place within you Elsa, the place that doesn't feel good, and find out why there is a part of you that thinks you deserve this because you don't."

Amira has mastered the craft of being cynical and harsh, and so delicious at the same time. But she's done lecturing for the day, done reflecting on this soap opera, knowing that Elsa will think she deserves this kind of treatment until she makes the decision in herself that she doesn't.

It's been made clear to Amira on many occasions during Elsa's three years of being with Simon that Elsa thinks it's somehow her own fault —that she is complicit in his bad behavior.

Then the thought crosses Amira's mind: maybe Elsa is part of making it happen? He's never been as impolite and douchey as he has been within the last year, so how could she not be complicit in some way? Elsa is the only one that sees him. Sometimes she wonders whether Elsa paying for everything makes Simon feel 'emasculated' —but then again, he never protests or howls in disapproval whenever Elsa does pays for shit, so how could it be that? Perhaps it's unconscious male behavior; he doesn't appreciate when something is given to him because he's lazy in every way —too lazy to get a job, too careless to do chores, too lifeless and mundane to be a good partner. Receiving assistance, especially financial, on a day-to-day basis is easy, almost nobody would say no to it, but it does hurt his male ego. Does Simon put Elsa down to feel better about himself? Maybe that makes him feel better for a minute or two, but definitely not in the long run, because no one can feed off of someone else's happiness by being cruel.

*

After Amira has left the bakery, Elsa is on the lookout for Gerda, hoping she will stop in after doing whatever she is doing out there on this frigid day. It's only two o'clock, but it's already getting dark outside.

Amira has gone home to work on a blog post that will call out her boss.

She told Elsa,

"I am leaving now to go tell the truth. I am going to write about how he and other staff members treat me at work for wearing my hijab the way I choose to."

Amira asked for Elsa's opinion and got her blessing.

"This is it, Amira. You have to do it."

Amira is going to write the article, post it on the blog tonight, quit her job tomorrow, and wait out the storm for the rest of the week. Her intuition tells her something is going to happen. She doesn't know exactly or even remotely what, but she knows it will be something, without knowing what that something is or means.

Elsa took the *kladdkaka* (chocolate cake) out and let it cool for one hour on the pie plate. After that, she's been serving it warm to customers all morning. What Elsa had been envisioning earlier is now happening before her eyes. Gerda, the aging fashion queen who always smells of alcohol is having an espresso. Getting eye contact with her freaks Elsa out. Gerda is the pure definition of loneliness mixed with great taste and money. She reminds Elsa too much of an older version of herself, which is frightening. To look at Gerda, you would never think she's got a drinking problem, but Elsa knows she does. Nobody comes in with alcohol breath every morning before noon and isn't abusing it. But damn, Gerda knows how to dress.

Gerda looks at her with conviction, smiling. Elsa smiles back eagerly and walks over to refill her coffee. Elsa does that for Gerda sometimes, and more. She'll slip Gerda a cookie or two, and today she is going to give her a piece of the kladdkaka —Elsa decided that when she saw Gerda approaching the bakery in the chilling cold. She is just doing what she would want someone to do for her if she smelled of booze and seclusion.

Elsa walks up to Gerda and serves her the cake. She finds Gerda sort of frightening; not in a mean way, but in an intimidating way that is quite the opposite of her own manner. The way Gerda carries herself when walking into the bakery is fascinating —if anyone on this face of the earth should have been an actress, it's Gerda. Just her presence is so wild and passionate. Marie had told Elsa about Gerda's family —they apparently own one of Sweden's biggest media production companies, SKAPA (create).

Elsa's mind is suddenly taken over by panic as the thought of her upcoming audition pushes to the fore —they have two auditions a year and she has submitted for the second one so she can audition again.

She thinks. "Why do I keep doing this to myself?" then she starts daydreaming:

Elsa sees herself performing at a big theatre one day and her father whom she's never met, walks in to see the performance. What if he somehow recognized the actress on stage and couldn't wait until the play was over so he could go backstage and ask the young woman if she knew of Edith Beijer —talking with a French accent perhaps?

Later he'd tell the young woman that he's been searching for her for years and years.

Judy, one of the morning regulars, brings Elsa out of her reverie:

"Hey Elsa, can I get a green tea, please? I need to go back to my worthless shop."

Elsa's daydream bubble is poked and vanishes in the air. Judy gets her free tea and leaves.

Judy is grateful to Elsa for always being open and willing to listen to her problems —and willing to donate hot drinks for free. Elsa feels neither here nor there about Judy, but still supports her when she needs an ear to listen.

Elsa walks over to Gerda to serve the cake, happy that Gerda came in today. She slips a note into Gerda's coat. The minute she does it she regrets it, but it's too late.

"Thanks," Gerda says, cooly.

Elsa thinks, "Is that all she is going to say after I've made all this effort?"

Why doesn't Gerda talk to her? Elsa has made so many attempts and with all the attempts, she feels frustrated. She wants Gerda to actually have a conversation with her, now. It's about time they did. Elsa feels she can help Gerda, she knows she has the capacity to do so —that's what she does best— helps other people while ignoring her own advice.

Elsa can't stop staring at her, thinking what a marvelous person is sitting there. She's not impressed by the money, they obviously have that in common, but rather impressed by her sense of fashion; cherry red lipstick, wavy dark hair, and most importantly, Gerda's eyes. When she comes close to Gerda and looks into her charcoal eyes, she sees how vigorously alive they are, as if they can speak a thousand languages. Gerda is preparing to leave the bakery having barely touched the chocolate cake. Elsa eyes her from head to toe while she's putting her coat back on, wishing she had the style to dress like her. Of course, Amira's style beats everyone for Elsa, but she can't help but feel mesmerized by Gerda too.

Shiny black boots with a beige blazer, a red Hermes bag, and a huge white fluffy fur coat. Fashionable, yet so different from the usual Swedish look (big white sneakers and jeans). Gerda does terrify Elsa, yet excites her in an unexplainable way. Elsa stands in the middle of the bakery smiling to herself.

"Vulnerability," she says out loud to herself.

Lucky for Elsa there is only one man left in the bakery, sitting at a table across from the fireplace, reading a newspaper and oblivious of her utterance.

Vulnerability is what draws Elsa to Gerda, she's figured it out. Vulnerability with a touch of mystery. Elsa is scared to admit it to herself, but she finds that mysterious vibe very intriguing and sexy. How can she feel that about another woman? For a few moments, the world stood still. Elsa's PMS symptoms went gone with the wind as she experienced a curiosity she'd never felt about another woman before.

"I wonder why she drinks so much, has she been through some terrible trauma?" She muses.

Without really understanding it yet, Elsa can fully relate to Gerda. They've both been through tough challenges in life, obviously. Simon is a sad habit and a bad addiction for Elsa, and alcohol is a sad habit and a bad addiction for Gerda.

"Gerda," she says out loud under her breath, cleaning up tables after the customers who have been visiting all morning.

Marie had also told Elsa that the fashion queen's name was Gerda, she had never heard it from the woman herself.

'Gerda', like the protagonist of Hans Christensen Andersen's fairy tale. "The Snow Queen". Gerda, who succeeds in finding her friend Kai and saves him from the evil Queen.

Sense

Gerda gets home in the early morning after having been out all night drinking by herself. She moves down her modern furnished hallway with flowers on the walls and sits down in a grassy velvet chair to take her boots off. Gerda lives alone with her white rabbit Lotta whom she lets hop around the apartment. Gerda has violent hiccups and as she holds her breath to try and make them stop, a crumpled note falls out of one of her pockets. She opens it as she sits back down in the comfortable grassy green chair.

Written on the note is a phone number with:

"Call me if you need someone to talk to. Elsa"

With a deep breath, she tries to see it as a charming action from Elsa's side instead of feeling distraught over the fact Elsa must have guessed the thing about her problem.

She thinks, "Elsa. The woman from the bakery. Her name is Elsa? Cool."

"Elsa" she murmurs. "Like Elsa Schiaparelli."

Gerda's favorite designer, Schiaparelli was an Italian fashion icon, now dead. Gerda loves to blend fashion with emotion. The impulse of the moment. Where life and fashion meet. Fashion has always expressed the darker times in history —conveys everything in every flash at all times. The greatest influence on her own fashion is the Dagmar sisters, three Swedish siblings that together created a Stockholm based label. Apart from their effortlessly elegant collections, Gerda has always been enthused by the fact they were sisters running their own label. She wears most of their clothes, watches all the interviews, and reads everything she can find about their lives. Gerda's relationship with the Dagmar sisters is protected and secure, they are not too close, so she can't get hurt by them —neither are they unreachable; she can engage with them from a convenient and safe distance. This is the closest thing to the sisterhood Gerda has ever experienced.

Before going to bed, Gerda thinks about how she would style Elsa —although she likes Elsa's jeans and white sneakers, she doesn't think it makes her uniqueness stand out enough.

"She deserves more," she says to Lotta under her breath.

Absorbed by Elsa's piercing azure sapphire eyes, she tries to put them together with outfits in her mind. What would blend well with Elsa's strawberry blonde hair, fair skin, and salmon pink freckles? Perhaps 'the cashmere lantern sweater' (the rose one) from Everlane, with 'Levi's 721' ripped high waist skinny jeans (rugged indigo) with Balenciaga's black *ceinture* leather ankle boots.

"She would look absolutely heavenly," Lotta hops away from her this time.

"Hey, come back."

Gerda keeps dressing Elsa in her head for different occasions. Party night on the town, 'Reformation's Christina dress' (the sunflower) showing a small peak of Elsa's breasts. Gerda loves how mini and cute they are, often wishing for a better glimpse during the bakery hours.

"Pathetic dirty all covering fantasy killing boring chinese factory worker t-shirt."

She glances at Elsa's note again.

"Elsa." smiling blithely and sensing a nasty headache coming on.

"Elsa, like Queen Elsa of Arandelle."

The Disney character from Frozen, she remembers cheerfully.

They had each in their own way thought of H.C Andersen's story, 'The Snow Queen'.

Originally the protagonist's name in that story was Gerda, but when Disney turned it into a film, they replaced the name 'Gerda' with 'Elsa' and changed the name of the story to 'Frozen'.

Gerda was too cool and oblivious of the past to know the character names of H.C Andersen's original story, and Elsa was too in the past and not up to date with the more recent Disney movies to realize the correlation.

For all heaven knows, this may be the spiritual connection Elsa has been feeling since first laying eyes on Gerda at the bakery six months ago. It may also just be a frivolous Hollywood coincidence. Whatever the case, whether childish, idiotic, or profound, Gerda and Elsa are somehow the same character in the same story.

Perplexed Outcomes

On this brisk Sunday morning in early March, two very content women are chattering away in satisfied tones about their friend Amira at the Swedish bakery.

In spite of Marie battling an internal sadness about her mother being sick, she doesn't let that get in the way of her feeling proud of a friend. Granted, Simon has been quarreling with Elsa all morning, but she is still ecstatic about seeing Amira on television.

They gaze at the screen admiringly, watching Amira being interviewed is delirious.

"She did it, she made it! Can you believe it, little swan?"

"I sure can," says Elsa through a grin.

Amira's plan to accuse her boss has led to her sitting on Jessie's couch, a locally famous Swedish journalist and TV presenter. For the occasion Amira is wearing a beige headscarf, exposing the front of her hair and demonstrating that she still stands by her opinions that she is going to do this whole Muslim thing in her own style —there is no 'correct' way to wear a hijab—

unbothered by her previous comment on her blog: "What the fuck is that...? Islamic Fashion?"

"What made you want to tell this story, Amira?" Jessie asks without emotion.

Amira answers in one excited breath:

"My whole life I always felt restricted and chained by people around me because of how I look, what my beliefs are, what I choose to wear, and how I choose to wear it, so I thought it's about time I stand up for myself."

Amira exudes confidence with an attitude so spirited it's almost certain her boss is going mad as a March hare at this moment. Her cheeky attitude is almost too audacious for this interviewer to handle, and her glimmering black long oversized blazer too exclusive and too rare to find and try to copy.

"What do you want to tell your employer?"

"I want to tell him and other people I've worked with to back off! I've never criticized their grisly clothes!"

Jessie quickly interrupts her and steers the conversation in another direction. It is getting too impulsive and gutsy for stoic Swedish news.

"Now that so many people have their eyes on you, what are you going to do?"

Amira quickly thinks. "I don't know, write a book? Isn't that what everybody does?"

She says it in a saucy sarcastic way, confusing both the interviewer and the viewers. Marie and Elsa can't help but find it amusing —it is entertaining when Amira mocks people in her arrogant manner.

Marie's worry kicks in, but she tries to swallow her concerns, but then she doesn't.

"I pray people don't think she's being too much."

"Well, save your prayers, this is the first time she's ever been listened to, she should sit there and destroy them one by one," says Elsa.

Marie comes back, "It may be that people need a good poke on the shoulder then."

"A poke in the eye with a razor-sharp stick is what they need."

Marie says proudly, "Look at her Elsa, who would've thought that Amira's blog would get so many shares?"

For all one knows this could be the result of the energy Amira was feeling before posting her blog. Something within her could feel the sensation of all this. What's that place that communicates with you without words —Intuition? Or is it something even greater? If the answer is yes to that, then what is it?

"I knew she'd make it Marie, I always knew." Elsa smiles.

Marie can't help but worry.

"We are going to have to be extra supportive from now on, a lot of attention will be directed at her. It's all very new and she won't necessarily know how to handle this."

"When have we not been supportive?" asks Elsa surprised.

Elsa remains calm knowing that if anyone can handle this scrutiny it's Amira. She's happy for her best friend, while in the back of her mind thinking about why she hasn't heard back from Gerda —and also about why she hasn't gotten out of her relationship with Voldemort yet. Couldn't someone just show up and save her?

Amira continues on the screen:

"I bet my boss feels bitter about hiring me, I should take him out to dinner so he can grasp what's happening here. You know, relax a bit. Get in tune and adjust to the changes that are happening."

Elsa beams at the screen wishing she could be more like Amira —reckless but grounded, feisty, and at the same time kind-hearted.

Jessie has started to loosen up a bit more, softening to Amira's personality.

"What would you tell your employer during that dinner?" amused, Jessie sits back on the couch, trying not to laugh.

"First of all, I'd order him some gluten so he'd get a stomach ache for the rest of the night."

Jessie can't hold it in any longer and laughs hysterically.

"So he is gluten intolerant? She asks while laughing.

The screen cuts to another reporter who makes a closing statement:

"It was late last night that Amira Diab posted an article accusing her employer of discrimination and what she calls 'Modern Racism'. The blog article has been shared over a million times online, and she is booked for an interview with Skavlan next week. Rumors about more international interviews are circulating."

The Diaries:
AMIRA

When the first person (I don't know who) acknowledged me on the internet then suddenly everyone did. Once a few people started noticing me, everyone did. The first time I appeared on television they finally started seeing me. Only then did I get a 'green light'. What is real and what is an illusion? Have I always been noticeable, or is it just now that I'm randomly getting all the attention I am worthy of? Does anyone really have their own opinions about people, and/or their art, or do they just go with what's trending at the moment? It feels like the latter. Where were everybody's consent and permission hiding before I started appearing on television? Am I really as smart and talented as the tabloids are saying? Or was I just a lucky person that posted something at the right moment? If I hadn't posted an article about my boss, would I have continued to be insignificant for the rest of my life? Is this what fame really is? Just waiting, and hoping for the 'right' person to like what you do, and then have everyone else jump on that same bandwagon? Maybe no one really has any talent until the 'right' people decide you do, and then that's what makes you relevant. Until that moment, you remain unsuccessful in everyone else's eyes.

What I don't understand is this: my whole life, I've tried to be seen for who I am as an individual rather than representing a whole religion, culture, or a country, but that has never worked for me. No matter what I did or spoke of, I was no more than 'the Muslim girl'.

Up until this moment, it has always been a battle to prove myself. Now I don't have to do that anymore because somewhere someone decided to share my article where I accuse my boss of discrimination in the workplace —and that someone was the beginning of the attention I was to receive thereafter. Never will I know who that first person was, but that first person was the reason I would have my voice heard.

What I've come to on my own is that fame is all about fleeting perception. We are all talented in our own ways, but we need to be in the right place, at the right moment, doing what we aren't meant to be doing. Only then will we be recognized. Elsa and Marie keep telling me that I shouldn't overthink it, that I should just be grateful that I've come this far. Don't get me wrong, I am grateful, but there is one little spot in me that's angry —just a tiny area. Why couldn't people listen to me or see me before this micro-fame of mine? Doesn't that mean people don't really have their own opinions? Are people too scared to make up their own minds before someone else makes it up for them? Who is that first person every time someone reaches success? That's what I am so curious about —who are these first people that decide we are worthy of a sprinkle of attention? Critics? In my experience, it was just ordinary digital wanderers. Perhaps that first person that shared my article could relate to me. In that case, great. I want people to relate to me on a bigger scale, but I would love to be heard on an individual level as well. For example, my third-grade teacher would always ask me weird questions and have strange assumptions about me and my family. Sure, my mother was always on to us, me and my younger sister Sara; she wanted us to get married, settle down and have children, but it was never because of religion, it was because of her background —and her generation. My mother grew up in Syria, and all she knew was that women get married and have children. That's what the women of her generation did. Don't blame her, it's not her fault, almost no Arab woman had more ambition or dreams about anything more than having children back then. There were no favorable circumstances for men or women during times of war.

My mother escaped the war wanting to start a family in Sweden, which she did when she met my Swedish father, of course, their cultural differences and my mother's raging temperament would break them apart early, and our father ended up abandoning us as toddlers. Both my sister Sara and I were born here. I love Stockholm, it's home to me, but sometimes people don't want me to feel that way. When I go back to Syria every summer my cousins see me as a Swedish woman. I come to visit them from a foreign country, I wear my headscarf differently, and I am not fluent in Arabic.

In Sweden, I am 'the Muslim girl' even though I was born here. I've come to accept the fact that I probably always will be the Muslim girl. Even after this dose of fame, I am just the immigrant girl who got harassed at work.

I am a woman whose mother doesn't know the Swedish language that well, and lives on welfare. Yes I know she doesn't have a groovy Swedish job, but she escaped to survive, is that so bad? Where is the crime? She had to start from zero without an education. It was hard for her to adjust to a new society. I have always loved Syria too, but when I grew into my early teens I started to look and think critically of my culture. I had empathy for it, but I knew it wasn't positive in a lot of ways, particularly not for women, which is why I decided to do it in my own singular and weird way. I know it might be out of sync with Islam, but it is me, and I love the way I find new ways to wear my hijab.

Today I feel like I understand both sides, the Syrian and the Swedish. I respect and love my roots now, and feel proud and happy that today I can create the life I want for myself.

I have never felt like I am allowed to say that I am Swedish.

"Are you Swedish? Really? You don't look like it."

Nowhere in the world am I allowed to be or feel what or who I am, because to the people around me I am what they think I am.

The hijab is one of the only things that keep me connected to my roots, that's why I chose to wear it. It makes me feel like I belong somewhere, and that I am not just flouncing in the middle of the ocean trying to find something to grasp onto.

I have tried to express these feelings for many years —to my parents, who don't understand a word of what I am trying to say —and to my Swedish friends, who won't let me be fully Swedish. Everyone but Elsa of course.

To the Swedes I say: it's not my fault that I was born here. And to my Syrian cousins: it's not my mom's fault she had to escape war and other miseries in her adolescence.

I do all the same things everyone is doing here that are born in Sweden. I speak the language fluently (strange that I even have to say that since I was born here). I have friends. I study. I am a good citizen —but not good enough to claim it as my country and call myself 'Swedish' it turns out.

"But I don't even see your mom as an immigrant."

Super cute —yes, thank you— but you know what, she is an immigrant, so why don't you see her like that? Is it really that bad to come from another country? This is what I mean by 'Modern Racism'. It's several layers down.

It's all around us, always has been really, and probably will be for a very long time.

Although I know my mom could have handled her transition to a new country a bit more elegantly, I also feel a tremendous amount of guilt over the fact that she had to run away. Being a young woman in a completely new and foreign environment is not easy. The fact that everyone expected her to learn to live all over again is unfair. Would you? If something happened in Sweden, or wherever you are, and you had to flee to a whole new world as a young person, would you start over again? Would you forget your own language and learn a new one just because complete strangers who don't care about you want you to? Probably not.

When my mom would speak Arabic over the phone in public places, she'd often get mean comments thrown at her.

"You're in Sweden, speak Swedish."

That to me is fascism. You don't just learn a new language at the drop of a hat, it's hard, especially in your mid-thirties, so back off.

I know I am not a refugee, nor am I trying to match my position or condition to one of theirs. I am just trying to share a piece of my soul here, so cut me some slack. You were the ones who shared my post, you were the 'first' people who decided that I am 'right' about something, so now that I have a platform, now that I am famous my feelings matter because you said so, right?

As I mentioned earlier, my mom is all about me getting married —or at least she used to be until my younger sister did get married. Only then did she get off my back.

*

Something happened to me a few summers ago. I was visiting Syria when suddenly my family decided —against my will— that it was time for me to get married. I was wearing a beautiful wedding gown and looking into a mirror I could see tears in my eyes running wild, and my licorice black mascara running free. My sister Sara tried to comfort me, knowing that this isn't what I want for my life.

"You have to do this Amira, you know you have to," she stated simply.

My mother walked past and gave me that harsh look she gives me whenever anyone disagrees or challenges her. That look makes me stiffen from the neck up.

"I can't do it. I can't do it, Sara."

I kept crying and mourning for myself when Sara grabbed my hand and said:

"Go."

I looked into Sara's deep pecan brown eyes, her round big eyes with short leather black lashes and her cinnamon-colored straight thick horsetail hair resting all to one side of her shoulder. The person that never expresses anything except through her eyes was looking into mine. Me, the emotional and selfish one, and she, the caring and unselfish one was telling me to leave. Sara was really urging me to leave and go live my dreams —not just to leave the wedding. She didn't say it verbally, but her eyes were screaming it.

I looked at her, knowing she'd have to tackle mom, a very intense mom.

"Don't worry about it."

Without putting my wedding shoes on, I got up and prepared for the leap.

"I'll cover for you, go!" she shrieked.

In short terms: I took off running down the beach in a wedding dress. I have no idea which beach, but probably somewhere in Syria. I get looks from curious people everywhere but manage to escape and get on a plane —I go back to Sweden, my home.

*

Sara got married two years ago. It was by her own will, she probably just didn't have anything 'bigger' she wanted to do in life. Who knows? Will she ever know? Did she give away the opportunity to dream to me instead?

Propitiously for me, from that moment on my mom backed off and stopped marriage harassing me after I threatened abandonment and a move to go live with my father.

After Sara got married, mom was happy as a clam that at least one of her daughters would have children. All of this made it so much easier for me to live. I could for the first time chase whatever I wanted without being terrorized emotionally.

Sometimes I think that it was Sara's soul's way of setting me free. She set me free from the many Middle Eastern standards and chains that are constantly passed on from generation to generation, mother to daughter, and mother to daughter. Her soul was willing to sacrifice itself so that I could leave and manifest my destiny. Maybe Sara believed in my dreams more than her own. It makes me sad to think this and sometimes I feel selfish. I am in fact selfish because the truth is, I would never have done the same for her. I will have to live with that for the rest of my life.

I guess when you don't understand why that first person made you relevant, you have to take a look at your life and decide for yourself.

Sara, you are the person that decided I was worth being listened to. That day of my wedding you said to me that you'd cover for me. I feel you did that in so many ways on so many levels.

Thank you my dear sister for covering for me. Without you, I would never be sitting where I am today. You showed me what real sisterhood looks like, what real sacrifice is, and what true love feels like when it touches a life.

Thank you, Sara. My *first* person.

Fika

Amira comes parading into the bakery a few hours after her TV interview. Elsa runs to the door and gives Amira a big hug. Never have they seen Amira so dressed up, she is wearing a sophisticated linen blouse under her oversized blazer, and a pair of black suit pants. Her beige hijab is blending into her set of clothes like the tip of candy corn.

When the four customers in the bakery see her coming in, they give her a round of applause which Amira takes in while reddening. Elsa walks her to the back of the counter where Marie is filling up on cinnamon buns.

"What an entrance!" Elsa says impressed, loving the fact she's here to see Amira blossom into such a powerful woman.

"I'm a star now, what do you expect?"

"Did you hear from your mom?"

"She called and told me not to crack too many jokes, be womanly she said."

"Oh."

"All she cares about is that I don't embarrass myself."

"You haven't."

"I know. Fuck her."

Marie walks up to them and embraces Amira without letting go, feeling like Amira has spoken up for so many women today.

"Let go, Marie, I'm a star now, things are going to change around here. You can't just hug me however you please." Amira smiles.

"Have a cinnamon bun dear."

Marie goes to the backroom to fetch a present she's been preparing for Amira all morning.

"Give me an ice tea, I'm thirsty." although Amira has a way of asking for what she wants in a very bossy manner, she doesn't really mean to.

"Do you realize what I've done? I'm finally putting people in their places. Especially that little 'ebn el kalb' (son of a dog). He will never bark at anyone again!"

Amira laughs, and Elsa tries to laugh with her without showing she's upset —but a true friend can see through a forced smirk. Amira changes the subject:

"Guess who's going to London next week?"

"Who?" Elsa asks.

"My brother in law and he asked me to come with him," Amira says, rolling her eyes impatiently, not giving Elsa one second to think.

"Me. I am going to London."

"To do what?" Elsa is still confused.

"To go shopping at Primark!"

The sarcasm is a bit too much for Elsa right now, and she is tongue-tied trying to figure out why Amira is going to London.

"I am going to participate in Skavlan!"

A popular Swedish-Norwegian television talk show hosted by Fredrik Skavlan.

"Are you joking?"

"Yes, I'm just being funny for no reason. I'm going all the way to London to go shopping at Primark. What is wrong with you!"

They both laugh excitedly, now that Elsa has figured out why Amira is going to London, and for the fact she is going at all. The two women are jumping around like giddy teenage high school girls when Marie walks back in with her gift: a basket with freshly baked blueberry muffins and a moist buttery almond sweet cake. Marie is a genius at giving sentimental presents, you can always tell she's put thought and affection into your gift.

She also hands Amira a small bouquet of mauve and amber-colored tulips. Marie put this petit bouquet together after visiting her mother, Birgit (who's getting worse) at the elderly care facility this morning. She bought the flowers from Judy's shop and used some old navy blue ribbons to tie it up after cutting the stems off with a very sharp knife. Like the flowers, Marie feels colorful but delicate today.

Amira receives the gift with grace but is eager to continue chattering with Elsa.

"But why London? I thought Skavlan was a Swedish show." Elsa asked.

"They shoot in London, New York, and in Stockholm apparently. I'm going to be touring like Jay-Z and Beyonce, you see."

"How do you feel, Amira?" Marie asks this attentively, trying not to show she's in her thoughts about Birgit, which she is.

"I feel so fucking alive. I did this cool interview, and it's almost summer."

"It's only March," says Marie.

"I know, but almost."

"Please let us know if you need anything, sweetie. I'll drive you to the airport."

Amira could tell something wasn't right with Marie the moment she got in. In fact, she can tell that there's something going on underneath with both Elsa and Marie.

"Marie, are you okay?"

No one says a word. Elsa is putting the tulips in water as Marie looks down at her cracked fingernails on her left hand with burn scars.

Amira presses "What is going on guys? Come on... I know I'm famous now, but I'm not some brick wall, I still have emotions so tell me what's going on."

Marie's emotional barrier is pried open and her delicate state is showing.

"It's nothing... It's mom. She's really doing bad, it's a matter of days now. Hours really."

When Marie visited her mom this morning, she was told by the nurses that Birgit had gone through a severe mental breakdown the night before.

"Mom's Alzheimer's has worsened over the past few weeks. It's not looking bright for her I'm afraid."

Amira is not that familiar with the disease, making her feel stupid and wrapped up in herself. Why hadn't she researched it knowing that one of her best friend's mother is diagnosed with it?

"Is there any treatment that can stop or reverse the progression, Marie?"

"I am afraid not."

*

Marie has been researching Alzheimer's constantly ever since Birgit was diagnosed two years ago. She knows there is nothing that can be done. Marie knew from the beginning that it would start slowly and gradually worsen over time. It started with the most common early symptom, difficulty with remembering events. Birgit had stopped asking about Cilla's drinking, she had completely forgotten about Cilla's problem. Before that point she would ask about Cilla's drinking all the time:

"Is your sister getting better?"

"Are you talking to Cilla about the drinking?"

"Is Cilla aware of the fact that she's drinking too much?"

All the concerned mother questions stopped. That's when Marie understood that her mother was truly slipping away. Marie knew that Birgit's biggest concern was Cilla and her drinking.

"Forgive your sister," she'd say. "She's your sister!"

But all that suddenly stopped and Birgit started acting strangely in other ways instead, singing Christmas songs in the middle of summer, going through horrific mood swings, loss of motivation —and the most shocking of all, the self-care issues. She stopped showering, stopped caring about anything really, and refused to walk an inch. The staff from the elderly care facility put her in a wheelchair, and after that, she never got out of it except to sleep.

Marie learned that the speed of progression can vary and that the typical life expectancy following diagnosis is three to nine years. Marie wanted to make the most of the time left with her mother. She wouldn't think of giving up, frequently visiting even though her mother was disappearing more and more.

The first time Birgit hadn't recognized Marie was one of the most difficult days on this gruesome journey. It was a year ago, on a hot summer's eve after a long day of back-breaking work at the bakery when Marie decided to put on a yellow dress and go see her mother, despite feeling drowsy from all the stress.

"Are you the nurse?" Birgit asked Marie in the middle of getting a haircut.

"No mom. I'm Marie… I'm Marie."

She sat down on the bed behind the wheelchair so Birgit wouldn't see the dread appearing like a storm on Marie's face.

"Who's Marie?"

"Marie is your daughter. Me, mom."

Marie sat behind her mom with tears gushing down her face. She tried hard to control her voice, desperately not wanting Birgit to hear the cracking emotion in her voice.

"Never knew of Marie." Birgit blurts.

"I come here all the time mom, I…"

Birgit interrupts in sudden rage:

"The lights go out in here all the time, the lights go out and I am left all alone in the darkness!"

Marie tries to talk through her tears, still not facing her mother.

"Mom, I come here all the time."

"Why didn't you come last Christmas?"

There was no logic anymore. No matter how hard Marie tried to explain who she was and what she was doing there, it never worked.

Marie knew it wasn't going to improve, and watching Birgit slip deeper into the disease was disturbing and utterly painful.

Marie would ask herself, "When would be the last time her mother would descend and never come back up again?"

The answer to that question was terribly closer than Marie could have ever imagined.

Six months later, Marie had been out picking Birgit's most treasured flower, Linnea Borealis 'Twinflower'.

Marie picked the flowers, planning to prepare them in Birgit's room so that her mother could enjoy the process of making the bouquet. She didn't care about the fact Birgit was very sick, or the fact that she hadn't been recognized for months —Marie was determined to give Birgit this experience anyway.

As Marie put the twinflowers in water, Birgit looked at her with a big smile:

"Twinflower, one for Marie, and one for Cecilia."

Thrilled, Marie put the vase down and sat close to her mother.

"Oh Mother, you remember, you do remember."

"The fire, the fire... The fire."

"It wasn't your fault."

Marie grabbed Birgit's face, looked into her eyes, and kissed her face, again and again.

"I missed you mother," whispered Marie.

"I was too hard on you."

Marie got so emotional she cried and laughed at the same time, embracing Birgit and kissing her again and again.

"Did we go to school near here?" Birgit said, slipping away from reality into her prison.

"Mother, stay, please stay mother, don't leave me again."

The staff heard screams from the room and ran in there to find Marie shaking her mother fiercely, crying out to her. One of the staff members had to grab Marie with all her strength to be able to pull her out of the room.

"PLEASE MOM, DON'T GO AWAY AGAIN. PLEASE!"

Marie had spent that whole night at the bakery, laying in a child's pose on the floor and sobbing.

Marie had gone from being Birgit's baby to becoming Birgit's mother, and then that night went back to being a baby again — only this time, a baby all on her own.

All Marie wanted to do was to lay in her mother's arms again and cry.

That day was the day Birgit never came up from the depths again.

*

Amira's concern doesn't hinder her from asking questions she doesn't really understand.

"What is happening to your mom? I mean, how is she behaving?"

Marie starts to cry when remembering the twinflowers day. Cilla hasn't returned any of Marie's phone calls for such a long time that she feels a sense of relief to have someone she can open up to, but all she can do is cry.

"I'm so sorry Marie," says Amira, reaching for her.

Marie can't stop bawling, but manages some words:

"She's having psychotic episodes, worse and uglier than ever."

Elsa went with Marie a few days ago to visit Birgit, and she respects the way Marie has cared for her mother throughout the years. Elsa had been there for many scary scenarios.

One time Birgit grabbed Marie's hair in a fit of rage and Elsa witnessed eyes captured in hate. It seemed like Birgit was possessed, but also in there somewhere deep down begging the monster to stop harming her daughter.

"Mom, please let go of my hair," her daughter begged her.

Elsa had seen with her own eyes how Birgit no longer recognized Marie. She was no longer part of a family, or of society. It had been a creepy experience for Elsa, but more than that she'd felt horrible for Marie. All of it had been way more horrifying than anything she had ever been through, even more chilling than the abortion.

Marie does not want to take the joy out of Amira's day, and she feels lousy to have taken the mood down so low.

"Please pardon me little swan... Please... I never meant to drag you into this."

Amira grabs Marie by the shoulders to show her that she means business, looking at Marie with an almost violent gaze.

"Don't you ever say something like that again, Marie. We are in this together."

Marie breaks down, even more, feeling simultaneously isolated and touched by the intensity of her friend.

"Why do I feel so forsaken?"

Marie feels deserted by her sister, even though she never really thought Cilla would show up during hard times —but that didn't stop her from hoping she would. She'd let her mind and emotions float, from feeling companionless to imagining she had all the support in the world from her sister. Marie often lived in a made-up reality in her head (just like she would when watching her films). She would picture herself in a perfect world, she'd imagine herself living vividly like that of a Carl Larsson painting, where Cilla would see her often, where they would call each other frequently and touch in —but every time Marie would come back to reality, there she would be forlorn, completely solo with no twin sister.

Both Elsa and Amira know that Marie feels the absence of Cilla, and they try to make her feel she has all the loyalty and support she needs from them, her young female friends.

Amira glances at the basket Marie had prepared for her this morning, taking out the almond nut cake to set up for a Fika (a Swedish social institution of taking a break for a relaxing coffee and cake).

*

The three women sit down with each other in front of the fireplace. Elsa feels tired and exhausted, both mentally and physically. Simon had fought with her all night, and her second audition is in April, only one month away.

There is nothing like a good Fika. A ventilation with your most admired women friends while sharing a little something sweet on a tender afternoon. This was a crucial part of each day for all of them. The Swedish almond cake texture is more like a cookie than a cake and gets its gusto from the almond extract and vanilla sugar. Marie's royal blue runny mascara has dried onto her cerise cheeks, looking like a piece of abstract art as she hungrily eats the cake with her fingertips made by her own hands. There is nobody in the bakery at the moment, so Amira takes her hijab off to relax. Elsa enjoys eating her cake. Marie watches the two young women earnestly, appreciating every second with them in Fika.

"I will miss my two little swans. With Amira's newfound stardom I foresee our bakery dates will become less frequent."

Amira can't envision that she'd ever stop coming to the bakery; it's the place where she feels the most loved and protected.

"These dates are the highlights of my life, are you kidding?" exclaims Amira.

Elsa can't comprehend why their bakery visits would become less habitual.

"I don't see why I would stop coming here. Besides, it's my job!"

Marie was always aware of the fact that Elsa didn't need this job to survive, so she was grateful that something within Elsa kept her on the job.

Elsa takes her pink apron off before brushing the almond cake crumbs off her stained white t-shirt. Her forehead is gleaming from sweat and her hair is greasy from skipping her shower that morning.

The almond cake dissolves like ashes in Marie's mouth which she politely shields while chewing and verbalizing at the same time.

"You'll be attending drama school my loved one."

This upsets Elsa to the core, don't these buffoons understand that she needs to be accepted by the school first?

"Have I been guaranteed a spot that someone is holding for me? Have I missed something?"

Her tone upsets Amira. She feels Elsa shouldn't be acting like this towards Marie who is feeling down today. Especially not after Marie baked everyone this astonishing cake. Like on most days, she defends Marie.

"Why are you being so catty?" Amira admonishes Elsa.

"Why are you being so mean?" Elsa snaps back.

"Who's done anything to you?" Amira is surprised.

Marie doesn't want them to quarrel so she jumps in the middle, carefully.

"What we mean to say is that it'll probably be fine."

"Probably?" Elsa asks.

"Yes, love. You are talented, you're Edith's daughter… She was one of the greatest actresses…"

"And that ended well," mutters Elsa.

Amira is even more annoyed with Elsa now. Who does she think she is?

"Did we wake up on the malicious side of the bed today?"

Elsa has a tendency to become very mean when challenged verbally, and snaps back:

"Did we wake up on the clownish side today?"

Amira is taken aback, not quite understanding where Elsa is going with this.

"So that's what I am to you. A clown?"

Hurt and confused, Amira gets up, needing to use the bathroom anyway. Marie feels blameworthy.

"I'm sorry Elsa," she whispers.

Elsa doesn't want to talk anymore, she stares down at her golden fork.

Marie offers, "Why don't you go home and get some rest? I'll close the bakery."

Amira comes back to find Marie alone cleaning the tables with a purple cloth and some citrus smelling spray. The bakery is closing a bit early today anyway because of work that needs to be done to the toilet plumbing.

It is also March nineteenth (The Spring Equinox), which marks the end of winter.

Without saying anything, Amira goes behind the cashier to count the money, the usual end of day ritual.

Amira finally asks, "What is her problem?"

"The mother talk is very hard for her."

"Oh please, it's not like she's Ted Bundy's daughter."

"It's tough for Elsa right now."

"It's tough for everyone right now. Always has been."

"Give her some time."

"I'm gonna give her a slap, I became a star today, she should show some respect!"

Marie and Amira laugh out loud together. Marie instantly feels bad for doing so.

"She's not well Amira, Simon is affecting her well-being."

"Simon is affecting everyone's well-being."

"It's worse now."

"Well, sorry but what did she expect? Caviar and rosé?"

"It can sometimes take time to get out of an abusive relationship, Amira."

"Oh come on, all she needs to do is to break up with him! Elsa is a free woman, she's not in Iran."

"It's easy for us to say, but she needs to reach her own limit with him, and that day will come, trust me."

"I doubt she will get out of it. She would've left Voldemort a long time ago if it was going to happen. She's a coward."

"Don't be so harsh little swan! We don't know what it means to be in a relationship like that."

"Oh please, save it! It's all about making choices, and right now Elsa is not making any choices! She's just walking around like a victim."

"Give her some time." implores Marie, seeing a hardness in Amira that scares her.

"I will trust me. Time is what she'll get from me. I'm not going to be the target for her misery anymore."

Amira has suddenly decided to take a well-needed break from her friendship with Elsa. She can't keep watching her best friend destroy herself. If Elsa wants to keep being abused then so be it, but she will no longer stand by and watch it because that makes her complicit. Amira doesn't think she is being fair to herself anymore. Why should she be part of this poisonous bullshit if all Elsa is going to do is bitch about it, go back to him, bitch about it, then go back to him again? Amira has been watching this same wheel in Elsa's life for more than two years now and she is fed up. The worst thing she knows in life is when people bitch about the same thing over and over again without making any necessary changes. Why the hell should she keep being Elsa's emotional punching bag? Is that what friendship really is? Amira's mom fled the freaking war, she's seen real problems, Elsa's problems are just so much bullshit.

An afternoon that had started with an incredibly sweet dessert, the encouragement of Amira's marvelous TV appearance, and the comforting of Marie's anguish, transformed and accelerated into a crack and fracture in what had become a bitter friendship. An afternoon of bitterness and sweetness. Bitter *and sweet*, not bittersweet.

Wayward Wicked Witches of Stockholm

It is early April, only a few days before Easter, and with plenty to do at the bakery before the schools close down and the family Fika hours begin. And a lot to do before Elsa's two days off before her audition.

The cute little Easter witches will parade around the streets dressed in junky scrapped clothing, red-painted cheeks, headscarves, carrying birch twigs decorated with colorful feathers. The little young witches will be going door to door giving out their home-made drawings, hoping to get candy in return. This Easter tradition is related to witch hearings that happened in Sweden during the seventeenth century when thousands of innocent women were burned at the stake for being 'witches' — Easter with a bit of Halloween thrown in.

Back in school, Elsa was taught that on 'Maundy Thursday' the witches flew off to mingle with Satan at Mount Blakulla. People would hide their broomsticks so that the witches couldn't use them to fly. Elsa thinks it's strange that a tradition coming from witch trials is now a ritual for children getting candy from strangers. At least that is some kind of progress.

This is a hard morning for Elsa, she started bleeding and had been up all night with violent cramps. The first two days of bleeding she can barely stand up from the pain, and she is so sick of her vagina interrupting her day by needing a new tampon. Elsa always thinks she needs to be bedridden after what feels like giving birth, and all the ache the abdominal cramps cause her legs. Is there an invisible sullen witch stabbing her in the pelvis?

Marie will be there within the hour to help Elsa prepare the smorgasbord —the bakery is quite famous for its family-friendly Easter buffet with numerous courses, and over the top decorations. They will be making meatballs, cold poached chicken with beet salad, lox, and tons of sweets all through the night. The Easter rush is almost as busy as the Christmas rush. Elsa will have to make the cinnamon buns by herself while Marie is out picking up Easter eggshell containers. When they're done decorating the bakery with birch twigs, feathers, and Daffodils they will fill up the eggshells with a mix of *godis* (Swedish candy), and hide them so the little witches can search for them when they come to give out their drawings of many cute little things.

*

Many Swedish loaves of bread and buns start with a basic cardamom dough and the vikings are known to have brought this spice back to Scandinavia from their travels abroad. For more than three years Elsa has been at the bakery, becoming a *kanelbulle* (cinnamon bun) master.

Traditionally, the portions of the dough are formed into beautiful shapes making them unique to the eye, and tasty to eat. Elsa has let the dough rise all morning and the next step is for her to knead the dough lightly. What two seconds ago was one chunk of dough is now divided into two halves and Elsa works them on the floured surface until they become smooth and crackless.

Looking at her handiwork she thinks, "Can everything in life be worked on until smooth and shiny?"

As Elsa prepares for the filling gathering the ingredients, the thought comes to her that she has tried everything when it comes to her relationship with Simon. He won't change. She needs to stop believing that one day he might. Is her relationship with Simon worth losing a friend over?

At first, Elsa accused Amira of being an 'unfaithful' friend when she had found out Amira wanted a break from her.

Elsa combines sugar and cinnamon then sprinkles the mixture evenly onto the rolled out rectangles of dough. She rolls up each rectangle like a jelly roll to form an eighteen-inch long cylinder. Using a sharp knife she cuts each cylinder into twenty-five equal slices.

After a few hours of letting the thought sink in Elsa started to understand Amira's decision, realizing that all Amira was doing was putting herself first —which is exactly what she should be doing as well.

Placing each slice in a paper cupcake wrapper on a baking sheet Elsa covers them all with a towel as they rise to double in size.

The fact that Amira is taking distance is healthy for her and of course, Elsa understands this intellectually, but emotionally she wants her best friend to be there for her. All the time.

Maybe Amira is doing this to teach her by example? Perhaps doing what Elsa should be doing in her relationship.

It all comes down to growing up, and it is time for Elsa to do that but the thought of leaving Simon frightens her. He's become an addiction —she can't be without him— she doesn't know who she is without him. At least that's what she's convinced herself of.

After forty-five minutes she preheats the oven brushes the cinnamon rolls with egg wash, and in honor of Easter she sprinkles the buns with yellow pearl sugar and places them in the middle of the oven with a timer setting of eight minutes.

While Elsa is carrying the Easter decoratives from the kitchen to the main room Gerda walks into the bakery. The sun has just begun to shine with its slashes of light matching with all the yellow decorations. The smell of cinnamon buns fills the bakery with a tsunami of a nutty toasted-like scent. It is unavoidable. Elsa feels great for a moment despite her greasy hair and gloomy forehead.

*

As Gerda walks in there is nobody else in the bakery because it hasn't really opened yet.

Seeing this Gerda asks, "Sorry, are you still opening up?"

"Yes, but you can sit down, don't worry about it." Elsa avoids her gaze.

"Thanks."

Gerda looks stunning as always, this time her hair straightened instead of wavy.

She takes her garnet shawl and dusty grey coat off, revealing that underneath she is wearing a silk leafy green midi dress with silvery buttons. Elsa tries not to stare but does so anyway.

Gerda's shiny black boots shimmer with a spark of sunlight. Elsa puts a big container of Easter decorations on a table close to the counter since Gerda sat down right by the front door. She doesn't want to make it seem like she wants to be right next to Gerda, which of course is exactly what she does want.

Gerda looks so vibrant, flourishing in her grassy dress.

"Do you think you could put some coffee on?"

Elsa drops an Easter rabbit made of wool.

"I did."

"Thanks."

Elsa feels shaky, should she really have put that note in Gerda's fur coat? Well, she is here, isn't she?

Elsa rushes to the bathroom to change her tampon, thankfully right before an emergency would have happened. The cramps have calmed down a bit. Elsa waltzes back into the kitchen in her nude-colored t-shirt and messy ponytail to get Gerda some coffee.

Gerda is just sitting there looking out the window.

"Thank you."

"You're welcome. You look great." Elsa blurts out and immediately regrets it.

She feels grotesque today and doesn't want Gerda to focus on her greasy hair and unattractive face, Elsa's pussflow often comes bearing the gift of these pleasant feelings about herself.

"Thanks," Gerda responds impassively.

The timer goes off and Elsa runs back to get the cinnamon buns out of the oven. They look golden and firm and she grabs a blue porcelain plate on which she puts a bun for Gerda.

"I was gonna say it smells good but you stormed off."

"Sorry?"

"Do you have time to sit down a bit?"

Does she have time to sit down a bit? —Of course, she doesn't. She has a gazillion things to do, to make and bake. But will she sit down? No question.

"I've got a little bit of time," Elsa says as she tentatively sits.

"Marie told me you were auditioning for a drama school in a couple of days, and I just came by to wish you luck."

Elsa tries to hide her boiling anger, she could kill Marie.

Why would Marie do this to her? Gerda is now another person she'll have to admit failure to when she isn't accepted!

Instead of roaring, Elsa says, "Oh she did, did she?"

"Yes, in the nicest way."

Gerda feels hesitant and a bit awkward, hoping she hasn't gotten Marie in any trouble.

Gerda likes Marie —likes her sentimental way of talking, and her quirky word usage; like 'my loved one' and 'little swan'.

"Look, I don't know if I was supposed to say that," Gerda says, looking directly at Elsa.

So now all Gerda cares about is Marie's feelings in this? What about her feelings? Elsa doesn't want Gerda to know how she's feeling.

"It's fine, I won't tell her, don't worry."

Elsa just wants to cry; she had a chance of being alone with Gerda, but now it's wrecked. Once you ruin Elsa's mood when she's bleeding, it's over, there's no way out of her feeling miserable. Nothing will cheer her up now. And on top of that, the cramps are starting in again.

"Well, I have work to do," Elsa says on her way to standing up.

"I'm so sorry, I won't bother you."

Gerda suddenly feels like she is imposing, one of the worst feelings in the world for her so she grabs her coat and shawl and leaves without thanking Elsa for the cinnamon bun, or reminding Elsa of the forgotten coffee.

The Diaries:
GERDA

L ike an emotional dagger, a short knife with a pointed raw-edged blade going into my stomach Anne's harsh words would penetrate my whole being without resistance. My dad had left my mom Alice for Anne, his co-president at his production company 'SKAPA'. Anne would never waver on an opportunity to be vulgar towards me, especially when nobody else was around. Not that my dad's presence would prevent her vicious comments. A bullet from the feminine is the strongest of them all, and when I was the age of eleven, Anne had made it clear to me that women were in constant competition with each other. Whether it would be about physical appearance, the attention from my dad, or my choice of interests. She'd be sure to find a way to put her own hurt at the hands of other women onto me. It was as if she felt safe to put it on me rather than anywhere else. I think my self-hatred started with Anne but ended with the others who would come after her.

I opened up to Alice (my mom) about what Anne would tell me, but it was as if I was offering her a cup of coffee she didn't feel like sipping on.

"Not now, Gerda, Thank you," she would say.

Of course, my mom had been hurt by women as well. Anne and she were high school friends and when it came out that Anne had been sneaking around with her husband for a whole decade my mom was forever bruised. Dad decided to go live with Anne and Alice never recovered. Alice prefers I call her by her name and it feels more natural to me anyway. One word can create separation, and that's what she wanted. She constantly, purposefully created an estrangement between us. Years of resentment and feeling like she wasn't a good enough woman because she'd been left by my father turned her life into a constant search for new boyfriends, always traveling and drinking. This was an easy way for her to occupy the mind and punish her own daughter for whatever bullshit other women had put her through. But then again, who knows how Anne's mother treated her? And what about the way Anne's grand-mother had treated her mother? That track could forever be followed back in time.

My late teens wouldn't prove to be any different when it came to trusting women. I became close to a girl from my fashion high school —Sally and I were assigned to do a project together and since we already did everything together, it felt nothing but natural when we decided to start a fashion label in school. We talked about ideas (mostly mine), and I gave her some of my notes to encourage her. She took all my ideas including a few drawings I had made of prom dresses and turned them into her own 'label'. When she presented this in class without me I felt like I was going to die then and there. Her presentation contained my drawings, and it felt like my heart and soul had been ripped out of me by my best friend. Everyone complimented her and she decided to do 'her' project solo. The teacher agreed.

Why did I let her do this to me? Why didn't I speak up? I was angry with myself for years. I still am. I felt like anyone could mess with me because I'd never stand up for myself anyway.

I went home, cried, and tried to talk to Alice about it. I knocked on her door —she opened it and told me she was busy before slamming it right in my face. She shut the door in my face at the moment I needed her the most. If my own mom treated me this way then why wouldn't everybody else? The drawings I had made were very close to my heart, so when Sally stole them and made them hers I felt like I had given away a piece of myself. I'm not sure I ever really got that piece back. Still working on it.

After that incident, I turned to alcohol to ease the pain. You may think I'm exaggerating but nothing I told myself would shake off the anger. Naturally, Alice was not much help. I confided everything to her in detail at one point hoping she would listen, but all she did was criticize and blame me.

"Life is not a fucking fairytale, Gerda. You want to get to the top, you have to kill."

Do we really have to step on each other to get to the top? I didn't want to believe that, but nothing proved me wrong.

I try to understand why women are constantly blathering about each other, followed by non-stop betrayal.

I promised myself to never trust a woman again. The alcohol made it easier to dim the pain.

At clubs I found like-minded people, there was extreme happiness released with alcohol that I had never experienced before. When people were drinking, everyone was welcomed. Everyone became happy and inviting.

Ten years went by, thrown away on drinking and messing around with different men. All the pressures of life disappeared when I met up with my drinking buddies. For a moment I felt alive, sexy, popular, and one of the cool ones. My drinking buddies and I were different but so alike —most were older; some younger, but still we all had one thing in common. The alcohol. The alcohol united us, made us happy, and helped us make friends. These people became my family. We hung out all the time. Day drinking, late-night drinking, and shank of the evening drinking. Everything became about the drinking — where we were going that night, what we were going to drink (beer or liquor or both), and what we were going to wear for the occasion. Of drinking.

One day, I woke up on the couch in my apartment with two of my closest 'buddies', Nicole and Harrietta, two women I loved and considered family.

Nicole, a thirty-five year old woman, had lost her job as a cashier at the local grocery store because of her drinking, and Harrietta had been kicked out from her family home at seventeen after she had been caught stealing from her mom's boyfriend (another mom story), but it didn't matter because I took care of them both emotionally and financially. That's what family meant to me.

I woke up and saw the front door was open, upon hearing whispers from my bedroom I walked in there to see what was going on. It turned out both Nicole and Harrietta had let two of their friends into my home, two middle-aged men, and it also turned out they were robbing me. I subsequently found out they had been stealing from me for years.

I sat up all night staring at my phone, looking at pictures of the three of us together, dancing, drinking, and having fun.

It turned out these people were never my family, it was all an illusion that I had created to make myself feel good. They had only latched onto me because I had money. I realized that these hustlers weren't the happy people I thought they were. They were just as lost and wrecked as I was. I knew deep down that hanging out with them was only temporary happiness, but it didn't stop me from living that lifestyle. We were all just absent minds and lost souls who hadn't created anything of value for ourselves. The fact that they'd been stealing from me hurt like never before. I think that all of this was meant to be because it made the transition easier as it allowed me to break free from them without any lingering guilt. I have not seen them for several years now.

Even though I poured out my heart and home to my female friends, they still felt the need to wrestle, to exclude each other, and go to war.

Alice, Anne, Sally, Nicole, and Harrietta —they had made the act of trusting women very hard for me. I tried, again and again, to confide in women, one after another, but every time I did I was always mistreated in the end. Every one of them was willing to stab me in the neck. I never wanted to keep women out of my life, and I felt like I was missing out on what I loved the most: intimacy.

Everybody seems to love throwing women against each other —the media, religion, laws, and men— and even women themselves. The fact we've been taught to not trust each other creates a huge rift, a scar between us. Our mentality as women has to change in order for us to have any chance of coming together as sisters. We need to understand that this suppression of true feminine connection, throughout lifetimes (if you believe in that sort of thing), has created rage towards each other that goes on and on.

We have turned our focus from the feminine mysteries within to targeting our looks, dreams, and personalities. The rest of the world and the men in it can go on as usual, undisturbed in their oppression because women are very good at holding each other down themselves. Why are women making it so easy for men to climb all over them?

That's why I don't blame all this bullshit on men alone — women are just as complicit— especially the ones that raise us and the sons. As long as we let this poisonous behavior towards one another go on, we are culpable in taking each other's power away. Is that really what we want to do? Or is it just instinct?

For many years I have experienced a lack of intimacy, a yearning for real female friendship. No matter what happens to me that longing never fully goes away. The feminine within will always keep searching for the kind of intimacy that only another woman knows how to give. Why else are most men so angry with us? Because we have a gift that we can only give each other. A gift no man can give, no matter what the price of the purse he has bought you.

I would drink to dull my sense of longing for a real female friendship but it would only go away for a few hours, there to meet me again in the morning. When I started talking to Elsa (known only as 'the girl from the bakery' to me at that time) I finally felt and acknowledged the grieving I was going through. The grief of not having intimacy with another woman had grown stronger and stronger with each passing year.

Elsa showed me what a deep and true connection with another woman is meant to feel like. It is nourishing and authentic, way deeper and effable than any relationship with a man. The feminine is mysterious, wild, and uncategorizable.

I open up to Elsa about everything now. My ideas, my thoughts, my emotions, and believe it or not, my drawings. I know she will never deceive me. She has proven to me that our friendship is worth more than trickery and deception. To both of us.

I think I met Elsa so that I could heal my past hurts with women. When women support women, prosperity occurs almost effortlessly and that's why there's a whole structure trying to dominate women. It is so frightening to the male mind.

I can now take a look at Alice's life and more deeply understand why her agony was passed down to me. Although I am her daughter her resentment towards women includes me because I am a woman.

The rage between women gets passed down to the younger women of the next generation. It all makes sense, why else would this constant clash between us never go away? Mothers pass it to their daughters, who then pass it down to their daughters, ad nauseam. My stepmother Anne's mother probably didn't shy away from expressing how useless and ugly she thought her daughter was, and for that, I feel compassion for Anne, even though she can fuck off.

When we untwist deceit and let our secrets unravel we blossom into who we are meant to be. Only then can we flow and expand across all the galaxies. At least I think so.

We are so beautifully connected, in many mysterious ways, the most mind-blowing one being: Every time I have lived with a woman, hung out with a woman whether it be my mom, Anne, Sally, Nicole, or Elsa. Our menstruations have always rubbed off on each other, tying us together by blood and having us bleed at the same time. Does anyone know why women start bleeding together when living under the same roof? It's overwhelming and astonishing to me that our cycles get affected by each other and start to harmonize together. I don't know what it means scientifically or biologically but in terms of spirituality I think I've figured it out, only in short:

When we let our hurts from other women unroll and shake out, they are reformed into the most magical of shapes. Your darkness releases unbend and disentangle itself from your soul and come back in the form of friends, happiness, and love for all eternity. This is truly my hope.

Expiry Date

E lsa feels alone and friendless. This is the time of the month when Amira knows exactly what she is going through. Amira understands her. Elsa decides to give her a call before people start bombarding the bakery.

"Hey, Elsa." Amira answers.

She was sweet enough to answer the phone, so maybe she's calmed down and they can become best friends again.

"Amira! How is London?"

There is a pause. Although it hurts, Amira knows she has to be firm with Elsa so she understands this break is real. Perhaps then Elsa will take a real look at her choices in life. Whether or not it's up to Amira to help her realize this she's going to take a break for her own sake anyway.

"Elsa… I meant what I said the other day. I still mean it. I can't be around this bullshit anymore, especially not now."

Elsa is speechless. What she really wants to do is to tell Amira about what Marie told Gerda, how they'll decorate the bakery for Easter this year, and how her period is making her feel batty again.

Amira continues, "I'm not going to tell you what you need to do anymore, I am done. You need to figure it out on your own."

Amira's words hurt more than walking barefoot on shattered glass. In fact, Elsa would rather do that walk than loose Amira.

"But we are friends."

"Being friends doesn't mean that I have to take on all your negativity, that's not what friendship is. That's not what being a friend means to me."

Growing up, Amira had been surrounded by many cousins and she doesn't know if it's a cultural thing, but she had to take distance from them because all they did was prattle about rumors, makeup, 'scandals' and gossip about each other. It had been painful to cut those bonds because they were family and she loved them, but she couldn't continue with the fakeness of it any longer. Amira had to break free from the toxic slander coming from her own family and since then she's been a far more jolly person refusing to get trapped in that kind of negativity again. Elsa's case is different, but it's still nonsense crap that can be turned around if someone really wanted to change.

"Fine, I'll give you some space."

"Fine." Amira hangs up.

*

Elsa turns the 'CLOSED' sign to 'OPEN' and prepares for guests to start visiting the bakery.

Marie walks in with two totes filled with Easter egg containers, yellow flowers, chocolate bunnies, and more festive decorations. She's dressed in a grey lavender long lace dress with a scalloped neckline, fluttery long sleeves, and has painted-on red cheeks with black dots for freckles on top of her facial scars from the fire. She is definitely dressed for the fun, but her amber blonde hair looks uncared for and neglected. Marie is behaving strangely, walking in through the front door which she never does (to avoid Judy mostly), and apart from the dress and makeup, she looks weary and overworked.

She says hello without hugging Elsa which has never happened in the history of their time at the bakery. Both women have 'things' going on in their lower parts today —Elsa's period is on its last legs, and Marie has an outbreak of herpes— The sores are painful, hence Marie is pantiless beneath her dress.

Marie starts dividing and cutting stems from the Daffodils without putting an apron on, which is also unusual for her. Her eyes look exhausted, almost empty, but she won't stop moving around swiftly, grabbing the scissors aggressively, throwing the plastic on the floor, taking a sip of water then spilling it.

"Damn it!"

She grabs a cloth from the table Elsa's been cleaning, wipes the water off the floor, then walks to the oven and eats a cinnamon bun from the platter next to it.

"Tasty."

Marie is usually a very calm and collected person, but today she is acting the opposite. Is this her twin sister Cilla? It's almost as if it could be —Cilla coming into the bakery to play the part of her sister for some unknown and creepy reason.

Marie accidentally cuts herself with a knife and sits down in a child pose, bawling her eyes out uncontrollably. Elsa is a very empathic person, highly sensitive when it comes to Marie, and just knows:

"Is she gone?"

Marie wipes the tears from her face with her bleeding thumb, leaving bloodstains on both dress and face from here till Sunday.

"Yes, little swan."

"When?"

"Last night."

"Why didn't you call?"

"I can't manage today, I just can't. The funeral will be held Thursday at two o'clock."

"Oh."

Marie looks at Elsa, really hoping she will be there at the funeral. With Amira in London, Elsa is all she's got.

"What do you mean 'Oh'?"

"My audition is on Thursday at two-thirty."

Marie is dying on the inside but is a master at hiding it.

"Don't you even think about it, Elsa. Do your thing."

"I'll come by right after. I swear."

"It'll be quick, only a few people are attending."

"Let's meet up afterward."

"Sure."

"I'm so sorry Marie."

Elsa is menstruating, Marie is bleeding from her cut thumb. They bleed together in an embrace, both confused and shattered for their own reasons.

Marie takes a look at Elsa for the first time today, noticing the dark circles under the eyes, she looks conquered and sad.

Marie walks to the front door and turns the 'OPEN' sign to 'CLOSED'.

Elsa feels a sense of relief thinking that this day must be cursed, it's been frightfully bad since she came in. Although Marie knows what is going on between Elsa and Amira, she feels it will be okay, but it is gut-wrenching nonetheless —the last thing she wants is for them to end up like her and Cilla.

"Are the cramps tough today?"

"It's okay," mutters Elsa.

"Are you still journaling and writing down your symptoms?"

"Only through an app."

"I wonder whether we could find you some natural supplements to take."

"It's okay," she says frustrated.

Marie goes to splash her face with some water from the sink in the kitchen, not really coping well with the fact Birgit is gone, or the fact that Cilla wasn't there and hasn't been for years.

"Let's call it a day shall we, little swan?" says Marie, water dripping from her face.

"I made the cinnamon buns."

"To hell with the cinnamon buns."

Marie throws the towel she uses to wipe off her face on the floor and Elsa grabs her backpack.

Marie helps Elsa with her jean jacket.

"Thank you, Marie... Sorry I won't make it to Birgit's funeral."

"Hey, you're off tomorrow so I won't see you for two more days. Good luck at the audition."

A crack in a long-lasting friendship and the death of a mother cause Easter to not be the same at The Swedish Bakery this year.

Microdose

Elsa has arrived at Tantolunden park. She's in the mood for a walk in the breezy sunset before heading back home. Elsa is drinking a can of beer as she sits in her car and puts on a big white knitted sweater, preparing for the crisp wind.

Tantolunden is a large park on the island of Sodermalm, where Elsa lives. There's a playground (empty now), a beach volleyball court (also empty), and a walking path that goes in circles. You meet the same people several times as you walk around it.

Elsa grabs a six-pack of 'Norrlands Guld' (a strong beer) out of the backseat of her car and sits in the front seat while drinking down a whole can. She looks outside while relaxing, observing two male joggers and a single woman power walking. She can't wait for them to leave so she can get out, sit on the dock alone, and drink. But first, she's going to take a walk. Elsa is a lightweight; she can feel a strong buzz after just one beer. Usually, Elsa doesn't drink much but she will tonight, hoping to escape reality for a while. The reality of her audition coming up, the reality of a friendship coming to an end, and the reality of Birgit's death. Elsa was never close to Birgit, but after all, she's known of her through Marie for over three years so she can't help but feel something about her death.

Elsa looks out at the sunset and decides to walk her buzz off —she doesn't like this sensation so she'll walk, hoping that it'll take her mind off things. The third can of beer comes with her as she steps out of the car.

The path is very appealing and green with its trees, grass plots, and dazzling water fountain in the middle of the circular walking path. She breathes in the brisk air, needing its cleanness.

The mind wants to go to the angst of feeling tipsy and out of control but Elsa stops her mind from going there, determined to walk it off. She takes an enormous breath from way down in her abdomen, smelling the scent of the grass around her in a way she's never experienced before. The colossal scent of grass hits her like a giant wave in the face, the scent of green never more alive for Elsa. With each breath, a new level of earth's fragrance is introduced. She takes a gigantic breath from deep in her lungs, and as blood oozes from a wound, the scent of wet mud seems to flow right into her nose. The scent is mixed with sensation, a thick and soft mixture of liquid clay blended with brown dirt. Looking down at the mud, she sees that it's both wet and dry in places between the patches of grass.

The water fountain is enormous to her right and stopping for a second she closes her eyes, the plumbing splashing water from four different pipes, and the gushes meeting in the middle to sound like heavy traffic.

As a jogger lopes past, she becomes aware of the three people around her for a moment, each moving at their own pace with a different distance from her. Smiling to herself, she keeps pacing around the circular path, meeting the same three people as they jog, sprint, and lope around her again and again. She imagines that the people around her know what she is sensing.

A young boy comes whooshing past on his bike making the sound of a giant snake crawling quickly towards her. Out of fear, Elsa grabs her diaphragm to try and calm herself down. She's learned through her acting training that this is the best way to catch your breath, to calm yourself down when in a panic.

Elsa feels connected to earth by all her senses, all working together, collaborating to give her an intense experience. Is this what senses are for? She decides to let go of the mind again — the mind that wants logic, black and white answers to everything.

When Elsa consciously connects her breath to her sense of smell, she experiences a different scent with every breath. Next, she takes a humongous breath and integrates it with her olfaction to form a sense of flavor. The aroma of someone's distant barbecue flows up into her nose. The slight smell of spicy seasoning tied with charcoal and chicken makes her yearn for food, the saltiness and zest leaves her craving greedily.

A chill wind invades her body, starting from the back of her neck, down to the knees, all the way to her toes, and into the ground. The wind went through her as if her body was transparent. Elsa catches another humongous breath inside a second breeze and is filled with the scent of freezing air. The wind strikes her again, and now she's cold. Giving in to all her senses, she invites the air to rush throughout her body. It feels like a tingle, times a thousand. The 'feeling cold' quickly evolves to what seems like a sexy massage from the universe. Every cell of her body shivers when the earth decides to make love to her. Along with getting chills all over her body, she can feel her clitoris get goosebumps. Elsa feels the beat of a strong regular rhythm pulsating steadily in her nipples and labia. A throbbing bliss. Her period cramps release into the ground as she feels one with the earth. Elsa cries, but it is not tears of sorrow but tears of joy. She feels the satisfaction and thrills the earth provides for her being a woman. There is comfort in being a woman because the earth is on your side. Earth is you, and you are earth. Earth gives birth and changes seasons, and so can a woman.

Elsa's intellectual mind bounces in to protest. What the fuck? Is she actually wet from the involvement with nature? What am I doing blending earth and sensuality? Humiliation, confusion, and regret come to visit her thoughts, but vigor takes over. Like relishing an appetizing flavor, Elsa allows herself to revel in the fact she's a woman. Women are robust and vigorous. Elsa is robust and vigorous. The fact that she's blessed with menstruation every month is a wonder. Never again will she feel remorse about being a woman. Never again.

Elsa is so much in the now —right now— the world feels a bit overwhelming. There are too many senses, too many detailed shapes and textures. She touches her knitted sweater, and the way it's made feels perfectly sewn and meshed. By and large, Elsa is often in her mind worrying about something, but now she senses everything instead of thinking about everything. She's in the now, now, now, now, now!

A massive breath from the upper part of her lungs sets her free from thought. Free from reflection, anticipation, and free from judging anything at all. She just is.

Elsa stops next to a tree, it's rough yet so friendly. The tree smells so earthy, a brew of sandalwood and tobacco. Without reason but only an impulse, she grabs the tree and embraces it with outstretched arms in a hug. It feels freeing —consoling to lean on something that can take all her weight without it feeling like she is being too much.

There have been times when Elsa has confided in people and felt like an instant burden. Elsa remembered one occasion when Amira had been in an outstanding mood before she shared with her the terrible things Simon had said the night before —Amira went from being on cloud nine to feeling furious and that made Elsa feel like she'd ruined Amira's day. This is why Amira wants space from her, she knows it. Is there no way to confide your own personal darkness to another human being without destroying their happiness?

A tree will never change its attitude towards you, no matter what stress and hardships you give it, the tree remains grounded and supportive.

Elsa keeps on hugging.

"Thank you."

You can always count on a tree, you can even kick it when you're infuriated, and still, the tree will remain standing there giving strength and warmth. Elsa kisses the tree.

"I'm sorry we hurt you so much."

The tree doesn't behave weirdly; it just stands there peacefully. This tree would treat Elsa wonderfully every time after this meeting. It's not the kind of creature that will go:

"Oh my god, you kissed me last time, and it was kind of weird, so now I am going to behave differently towards you."

"Thank god for trees," she whispers to herself.

Elsa gets startled by someone playing with a ball across the park near the water. It sounds like one huge spit every time the ball hits the ground, a big spit mixed with a slap.

The only jogger left in the park passes her with an interesting speed, not fast nor slow but somewhere in between. Elsa closes her eyes to sonically explore the rhythms around her. If it wasn't for the fact she'd just seen the jogger a split second ago, his beat could easily be the same as a horse's gait. That, or a man with four legs, same pattern, same flow, same tempo —at least that's what it sounds like when you've had a bit too much to drink.

Another wind hits the back of her neck, every cell in her body pulsates. She can't tell if she's feeling cold or just being present. Maybe being cold is just the wind's way of connecting with us humans. When she's conscious of the wind it's a very sensual feeling, when she's not conscious of it, the wind feels like getting a slap right across the face with a cold touch.

Elsa's ears start to change color; she can feel that they've turned ruby red. The feeling of ears going sour from the wind. She guesses that it is cold after all. But where are these contemplations coming from?

Elsa passes the fountain again, this time the water sounds like the chattering of two hundred people or the sound of an airport terminal. The tempo of the chattering is too fast to hear what anyone is saying.

The cramps are coming back, she doesn't want them to and she'll do anything to stop them.

Elsa lays down on the lawn and listens to the crane birds near the lake. These birds usually arrive here in April. Great timing. Their chirping sound is like the sound of a pistachio nut opening but with a higher pitch when the shell breaks. A more beautiful sound of course than pistachio. What is she thinking?

Is this why people take long walks in the woods, out in nature? Do all nature lovers feel this way? Is it a conscious or a subconscious impulse?

Most likely everyone feels the way she is feeling, but they can't put the sensations into words. Neither can she.

In nature, she is in her body more than anywhere else. She lets go of the mind and lets her body guide. Elsa's body is alive but her mind is on vacation.

A crow makes a sound startling her again. Even in nature, there is the light and dark, as Marie had explained to her. Elsa is having a wonderful experience mixed with moments of doubt and fear. Is there a price to pay for everything? Even in the middle of nature? Of course, there is a price.

Elsa walks out to the landing pier, chugs down the remaining two cans before laying down to rest for a while. The sun sets and it gets dark. As Elsa is laying there she glances at the water. It is pitch black and frightening. She's cold and has bled through her tampon, but what is she to do?

Her mind pays a visit and decides to pair her with the devil. Anxiety rises, lustiness quickly turns to despair —the price you pay for drinking. Her mind plays through a bunch of scary snippets. Her memories of 'the horrible nights' come back and as if outside her own body she sees the young little girl she once was. That little girl had to endure tremendous amounts of pain because her mother had abandoned her. It would never have happened if Edith had been there to make it stop. Like a hologram displayed in front of her, she sees the day she went through the abortion alone, filled with panic. A nightmare.

Elsa stands up and tries to remove the screen she thinks is there. She is in ineffable torment.

"Leave me alone. Go away."

Elsa starts hyperventilating unable to calm herself down. The fright builds and she plunges right into the dingy water off the pier. Incapable of swimming in this condition she starts swirling beneath the surface, tries to swim in the right direction until there is no right direction. A swirling black and freezing tunnel is all Elsa can comprehend. Unable to understand where the bottom or surface is she starts making uncontrollable movements with her arms and the legs. The terror, the shock, and the powerlessness is real, and very much in the now, now, now.

Elsa's movements start to become less and less frantic. She is fading away when she sees what seems to be a dying flashing light with a half-lit bulb. She feels at peace.

Elsa sees the people that love and adore her, seeing them in her mind's eye; she can feel them too.

She sees Gerda's dark eyes looking into hers. She knows Gerda is lonely, knows she has never had a friend before, but now feels that Elsa and she might become something.

Marie's presence is felt, she can hear her voice and see her amber blonde frizzy hair.

"If it wasn't for you Elsa, the bakery would've shut down a long time ago."

Amira's distressed face appears to her, the clearest vision of them all. She can feel that Amira is worried sick about her.

"If it wasn't for you, I'd never had the courage to do anything I was meant to do."

Elsa keeps swirling around slowly in the water, peaceful. Is she dead?

Everyone Elsa just saw or felt disappears like a computer shutting down after water has been spilled on it.

A blonde woman in her early thirties swirls towards her. Elsa recognizes the face.

It's Edith, and Elsa tries to touch her face but can't reach her. Edith smiles.

"I'm here Elsa. I've always been here."

Edith comes closer, letting Elsa feel her nearness, reaching out her hand to touch Elsa's freckles:

"Just like mine."

Edith expresses with pure emotion what a grim and empty life she would have lived if it hadn't been for Elsa.

"I spent my life trying to find meaning. When you were born I found it."

Life without Elsa would have been dark and unbearable for Edith. Before having her baby, Edith had won the finest awards an actress could dream of but still couldn't find happiness within herself. Edith tried every drink, every outfit, and every city in the world, but nothing worked until Elsa was born on February 4, 1993.

When it was ruled that Edith had to give up Elsa to social services life became gruesome and dark again. She couldn't bear going through the horrid emptiness again.

"I'm sorry Elsa. Please forgive me. Please."

Swirling in the deepest part of the pitch dark water, Elsa feels at peace.

She suddenly comes out of this waking dream, her body shaking violently with energy that doesn't feel like it's coming from her. Will is firing up in her belly, the will to survive.

Like waking from a nightmare Elsa opens her eyes and takes control over her body.

She can see the dock, swims towards it with a strength she didn't know she had, grabs the dock, and pulls herself up with a force she's never used before.

Elsa sits up on the pier and coughs uncontrollably. She can't wrap her head around what just happened. Was she dreaming? Did she die and come back from the dead?

She feels like an alien, can't recognize herself because she has never had any of these perceptions before. Edith loved her that much? What?

Something down there saved her, but who? Elsa doesn't believe in God.

Freezing and trying to catch her breath Elsa throws up on the surface of the dock, then begins to try and stand up, but it's tough. Her legs are trembling and she is highly emotional. A sense of gratitude has invaded her whole being.

While walking to her car Elsa falls and hurts her right knee. The last thing she wants now is to be alone. She sits down inside her car and puts the heater on.

Elsa is confused, but at the same time very happy. Her intuition tells her to check her phone, and thank god for that intuition because there is a text from Gerda:

"Are you okay?"

When Gerda left the bakery that morning she felt gross for having walked out on Elsa who'd shown so much warmth and care for her. She felt disgusting and selfish. Gerda was in fact worried about Elsa. Why couldn't she just put the past in the past and learn how to trust women again? Gerda didn't know.

Elsa decides to text Gerda back without caring what she'll look like:

"Do you think I could come by?"

Elsa puts the phone away and starts to sob uncontrollably, feeling free from harm. Happy. The 'vision' in the dark water had shown her how much she really means to people. Why would anyone let go of that? The influence she has had on people truly means something to her.

But who, or what had shown her all those things? Why? It must be something the mind can't comprehend, just like all the sensations and scents of nature. Elsa wants to put it into words, but can't. She wants to tell Gerda, but won't. No one would understand, she'd just sound crazy. But Elsa will forever know she observed something mystical this evening, and she wants no one, absolutely no one, to ruin that magic for her.

She decides to never tell a living soul about what happened to her today, because not only did she experience both the light and the dark, she saw it and she felt it palpably in her own body. She knows they both exist in parallel in this universe. The truth is in the paradox.

Chick Flick

It is always midnight in Gerda's eyes, hemmed in as they are by slight crow's feet. Those eyes make it hard for anyone to figure out what she's thinking at any given time. Elsa rings the doorbell to Floragatan fourteen, Gerda's street address, and a mysterious looking Gerda dressed in a greenish-blue Japanese satiny kimono comes to stand in the doorway.

"What happened to you?" Gerda asks, looking intently at Elsa.

Elsa smiles with gratitude, there is nowhere else she'd like to be right now, and she can't wait to get into some new attire (hopefully Gerda will lend her some).

Gerda's breathe screams of alcohol.

"I kind of went for a swim," says Elsa indicating her wet clothes.

"You kind of went for a swim?"

Elsa steps inside and takes her sneakers off. She's freezing and repulsed by the fact her tampon has been inside her way too long.

"I'm gonna get you a towel and some clothes," Gerda offers.

"Much needed, thank you!"

Elsa takes her white knitted sweater off and walks behind Gerda towards the living room. Gerda's apartment is an ideal of flawless Scandinavian style. A brand new modern condo with exposed wood beams and a wooden staircase that tells Elsa this is a two-story affair.

Gerda's interior design is warm and cozy with big white walls that she has filled with huge colorful abstract paintings. There are details of a rustic approach, the floor lamps and the tv stand have metal legs. The place has high ceilings and big windows, the tallest windows Elsa has ever seen in a Stockholm apartment —she glances out the windows on her way to the bathroom, it is dark out, but she can see the hint of a neat balcony.

Gerda comes back out and hands her a silky white robe, a towel, and two different sets of outfits to choose from. She leads Elsa through the bedroom to the bathroom and shows her where she keeps her skincare products. There are a lot of them, every girl's dream, all the brands, shapes, and forms possible. If only Elsa knew how to use any of it.

Gerda's bathroom is huge, the marble and mirrors are all that Elsa can take in right now, she's burned out and smells like piss.

"Sorry about the smell," says Elsa embarrassed.

"Don't worry about it. Take your time."

After walking out of a hot shower, Elsa puts on a pair of cotton slippers to go with the ivory silk robe Gerda gave to her.

Elsa's hair remains wet and messy, but most importantly she's got a new tampon shoved in. Right before getting in the shower, she'd asked Gerda for one, and without it getting weird or uncomfortable she had shown Elsa where she kept all 'that stuff'.

Elsa finds Gerda feeding a white rabbit. She looks at this curiously, wondering why Gerda would have a rabbit running around her apartment.

"This is my rabbit, Lotta."

"What's the occasion? Easter?"

"No, she lives here all year round."

Lotta is Gerda's only female friend. When Elsa bends over in an attempt to touch Lotta, the rabbit scuttles away.

Gerda smiles. "You must be hungry?"

"I'm starving, but don't worry about it, I'll grab a fruit or something."

"A fruit or something when you're starving?"

"Sure."

"I ordered Chinese, it'll get here in twenty minutes or so."

Elsa asks if Gerda has any pills for period pain, which she does. The cramping will be better by tomorrow, at least Elsa hopes so.

"I'm boiling water for tea," states Gerda.

Gerda has added some unusual color to her traditional Scandinavian kitchen, the cupboards are mint green, a color Elsa has never seen in a home before, let alone in a kitchen.

Gerda opens up the cupboard and takes out two silvery cups with emerald green floral patterns. It's clear that Gerda loves green. She wears it, has it in her kitchen, her cups, and there are vases of eucalyptus in both the kitchen and bedroom.

Elsa can see that Gerda is blessed with an amazing talent for interior design. They sit down at her square wooden dining table with four metal chairs around it. The entire apartment is stylish with cushy details resembling Gerda's personality.

She pours the boiling water from a raven black ceramic handmade teapot into the two matching silvery cups.

"This tea is organic, it's a leaf tea with chamomile and orange something."

"Orange something, thank you," says Elsa.

The two women are nervous, which results in them repeating each other's words —mostly Gerda since she is the one that's the timidest, although she covers it well. Gerda is aware of how edgy she feels about being in the presence of another woman again.

Elsa feels very taken care of, excited to get to know Gerda more. Lotta jumps around the apartment however she pleases.

"I hope it's okay I came over," says Elsa, breaking an awkward silence.

"Totally okay."

"I don't want to seem weird or anything."

"You don't come off as weird to me."

Elsa glances at the kitchen island made of white marble trimmed with mint-green wood.

"I love your home. I knew you'd have a great stylish place."

"You did?"

"Yes."

Elsa watches Gerda in her green kimono, she gazes at the emerald green details on the sleeves with blossoms and circular patterns, a dazzling design. Gerda notices:

"I bought this when I was a fashion student visiting Paris."

"Would you mind it if I stayed the night?" blurts Elsa.

Elsa is one of the most alluring young women Gerda has ever met, her eyes like a bottle of the French liqueur 'chartreuse' blended with the color of sage, creating a grey-green bewitching eye color. She is mesmerized by Elsa's natural magnetism. What's so sexy about Elsa is the fact she doesn't know how extremely beautiful she is, which just adds to her allure. And Elsa has not even fully grown into her beauty yet.

Gerda is without a doubt going to give her a crimson red lipstick that will make her eyes and freckles stand out more.

"What is it?" asks Elsa coyly.

Elsa is not blind to the fact she is being eyed by Gerda. Does she still smell bad? Her hair is drying, and the strawberry blonde aspects are peeking out of the darkness more and more.

"Nothing."

Gerda blows into her teacup and the steam blows right back into her face, causing her to cough slightly. She moves the cup away.

"Are you okay?"

Gerda just looks at her in silence with a slight smile.

*

After eating an enormous amount of chicken chow mein, glazed pork belly, and biang biang noodles, the two women have thrown themselves onto Gerda's L-shaped velvet pencil-grey couch and put on the movie Madicken, which features a fictional character created by Astrid Lindgren (the movie was Elsa's choice). Elsa used to watch reruns of the Madicken tv series from 1979, as well as reading the book with her mother Edith. Madicken is an upper-middle-class girl who lives with her parents and younger sister Lisbeth in a small town in Sweden. While Madicken is seen as an untamed young girl, many of the locals regard her as the 'spoon-fed little spoiled girl' —her sister Lisbeth admires Madicken's stubbornness and grows up to be opinionated and headstrong just like her sister.

"So why do you think your mom made you watch this? So that you wouldn't grow up to be a selfish little rich girl?" asks Gerda after they've watched nearly the whole movie.

"Don't talk shit about Madicken! She's a spoiled rich girl, but with a caring heart."

Gerda had given Elsa the most beautiful blanket Elsa had ever seen to throw on and keep her warm while watching the movie —a splendid peach velvet blanket with tassels on two of the long ends. Elsa feels like she's enjoying a stay at a lavish five-star hotel.

"Why are you being so nice to me?"

"I'm inspired by Madicken," says Gerda with a sly grin.

Gerda's neighbors can hear their audible laughter as they watch the movie because she had opened up the balcony door when the fireplace made the temperature in the room rise too high.

Elsa chuckles, but gestures for Gerda to stop howling so loud.

They watch a scene with Madicken and one of her poor neighbors, Mrs. Nilsson, a woman that sells her body for research (to be given to the town's doctor after she's dead), and in exchange is given money from the doctor in advance. Later on,

Mrs. Nilsson comes to feel bad and scared about the fact she won't be given an honorable funeral. Madicken wins the lottery and buys Mrs. Nilsson's body back from the doctor. The poor family exclaims and cries out in joy when they hear what Madicken has done for their mother, especially Abbe, their one and only son with whom Madicken has formed a close friendship.

"How come she's so nice anyway?" questions Gerda.

Gerda doesn't remember watching or reading these stories. Although fascinated by Madicken's kindness, she finds it hard to believe that anyone would be that generous in real life. Although she herself is that generous.

"It's because her father is a socialist and the editor-in-chief of their local newspaper."

"So what?" Gerda is unconvinced.

"Well, he is constantly telling Madicken stories about discrimination and unfairness in society."

"So he's a rich socialist in the nineteen hundreds?"

"Yes."

Gerda ponders for a moment, then says, "Cool."

*

Gerda left Elsa sleeping on the couch throwing an extra blanket on top of her just in case. Then Gerda sat awake in her bedroom with a glass of wine.

Her king-sized bed frame is made of sustainable pine wood, the most common tree in Sweden. The frame is secured with strong metal brackets, and the stitched lavender linen duvet cover matches with the soft mauve subtle stitching of the blanket. She doesn't have the typical nightstands on each side of the bed. Her bedroom is minimal yet cozy. Next to her bed, she has a copper floor lamp crafted from brass with a marble base. At the front of the bed is a 1940s yellow boudoir shaped chair with matching brass legs. Aside from that, there were only two big green palm tree-looking plants, and string-lights dangling down from the big window across the room.

Gerda wonders what Elsa's intentions may be? Elsa doesn't seem to be an evil person, but then again she's been dead wrong about women before.

*

When Elsa wakes up on the couch the next morning —Lotta, is sitting by her feet, finally softening to her a little bit.

The sun is shimmering through the windows with a punch.

Elsa looks at the eggshell-colored fluffy carpet that Gerda has covering the whole living room. She puts her feet on it carefully and can feel last night's drinking offering a visit in the form of a headache.

She grabs her phone from the wooden coffee table in front of her —seven missed calls from Simon. But fuck him. She's got a monologue to memorize and an audition to prepare for. Searching around on the table for a charger, she looks at the glass vase placed in the middle of it. A vase with a dried canella berry bouquet. It is artfully arranged and looks like a decorative touch that's always in season. Judging by Gerda's plants and flowers, she seems to like them dried since this is the third one Elsa has seen —the second was a red eucalyptus bouquet in the bathroom, and the third a dried ochre.

Rambling through the pile of clothing Gerda gave her last night, Elsa puts on a flamingo-pink velvet knit mini dress with a v-neckline. It seems that Gerda treasures velvet.

Elsa's hair is messy and she can't find a hairbrush in the guest bathroom. There is nobody in the living area except Lotta, who is sitting on a wooden stool next to the tv. The rabbit's intense look tells Elsa she is being patrolled and spied on.

The sound of a sewing machine can be heard coming from a room down the hall she hasn't been to yet, so she starts guardedly walking toward it.

The melody of the machine stops just as Elsa peers into the room, looking through the doorway.

Gerda is sitting in what appears to be her workspace, highly focused on the controls of the sewing machine. She turns the knob which changes the type of stitch she is doing, going from a straight stitch to a more advanced pattern.

There is a french door that opens onto a petit balcony, with only one chair outside. A white porcelain-covered foldable metal chair with an ashtray on it.

There are all kinds of art craft material everywhere in this simple but messy room. Gerda is sitting in a green velvet chair with metal gold legs (like the one in her hallway) positioned in front of a distressed wooden table that supports the sewing machine.

To Gerda's left, there is a female mannequin on a wooden tripod, with small pieces of paper stuck into it with pins.

Gerda presses her foot on the pedal and continues sewing what looks like an apricot-colored crocheted sweater. She has her hair up in a half-bun, which makes her look more matronly. She wears bright Levi's jeans and a beige blouse with cute dots on it. Gerda wears the more mature hair effortlessly. Next to Gerda is a half-full glass of white wine.

Elsa says, "Good morning."

Gerda screeches out in fear:

"AHHHHH what the fuck?"

Elsa jumps in, "I am so sorry, I'm sorry I didn't mean to frighten you."

"You scared the shit out of me, no one has been here but Lotta and me for years!"

There is so much Elsa wants to know about Gerda — obviously her dad owns a big production company, but why is she so alone? Why does she drink a barrel of wine every day? And where are her female friends? Is she deliberately keeping herself segregated from the flock?

Gerda can see that Elsa is eyeing her glass of wine.

"It's for the hangover."

"I get it."

"You look good in the dress."

Gerda starts playing around with the spool pin —the metal pin that sticks out of the top of the sewing machine and holds the thread.

"You can keep it."

"No it's fine, I'll give it back later."

"You can keep it," insists Gerda.

Gerda's tone is very determined, and Elsa wouldn't want to go against anything Gerda says when she is being persistent.

"That's so cool, thank you."

Can you instantly take back what you say? Because Elsa thinks she sounded like the biggest dork saying that the way she just did.

*

The two women stand across from each other leaning on the marble kitchen island in Gerda's mint green space.

Elsa inquires, "Where do you get your interior design inspiration from?"

"Fashion magazines, Pinterest."

"Same with fashion I take it?"

"Fashion for me has always been a personal art form. I guess my artistic expression comes through clothes and interior design. Sometimes through drawing."

"Impressive, I wish I had more of a fashion sense."

Gerda continues, "You can always hide your emotions behind a great outfit, no one will ask questions about your well-being or refer to your alcohol breath if you're wearing a striking set of clothes every day."

"Really?"

"Sometimes you can even fool yourself."

The vulnerability that Elsa has sensed in Gerda since the first day they met is finally showing itself. She has tried very hard to make Gerda feel like there is a safe space for her to open up.

"Why wouldn't you want anyone to question your well-being?"

Gerda answers with a happy expression which Elsa finds mysterious. The most you get from examining Gerda's face are two secretive jet-black eyes focusing on you intently.

Elsa decides to be adventurous, which Gerda unintentionally brings out in her. Elsa feels herself become gutsier and more forward in her presence.

"Tell me something nobody knows about you."

"You first," challenges Gerda.

"I asked first."

"I might move to New York after the summer."

"Why?"

"I want to start my own fashion label... And maybe join Alcoholics Anonymous."

Elsa can't tell if Gerda is being sarcastic or serious.

"Are you close to your family?" asks Elsa.

"Not terribly."

Elsa has a sip of the water. Her headache doesn't feel like it's getting better —menstruation mixed with a hangover isn't a walk in the park.

"It's your turn," says Gerda.

"I don't know what to tell you."

"Are you Edith Beijer's daughter?"

"Yes."

"Is it true she had a Borderline Personality Disorder?"

Elsa feels like someone stabbed her in the neck. Where is Gerda going with this? She obviously knows who Elsa's mother is and what condition she was in at the time of the accident.

"What were you doing swimming with all your clothes on?" Gerda continues.

Gerda is going all-in with her questions, too curious about Elsa to back off.

After a pause, Elsa simply says, "I had an abortion last year."

"What does that have to do with swimming?"

"I was drinking... Memories just started coming up so I thought I'd take them for a swim."

There's a silent moment before they both break into laughter. Elsa's dry humor really takes Gerda by surprise.

Elsa just asks, "Are you a lesbian?"

"Are you going to tell me about the abortion?"

"Is that why you drink?"

"Do you regret it? Is that why you threw yourself into the water?"

Elsa wonders if Gerda is just being curious, or if she is being mean? Why is she so harsh all of the sudden?

Gerda wants to make Elsa talk —she doesn't mean to come off too jarring, but she wants Elsa to open to someone. That someone being her.

After Elsa doesn't answer, Gerda says, "I'm sorry."

Gerda feels like she is becoming her mother, instantly repulsed by the way she has approached Elsa with these questions.

"It's okay," Elsa responds blankly.

"Are you hungry?"

"Not yet."

*

If it hadn't been for the abortion, Elsa would've had a two-year-old today. Although not hyperthymic, she can recall the day of the abortion in very specific detail.

After making the decision she wasn't mentally or emotionally fit to raise a child, she called doctor Gunilla to schedule an appointment. That decision was hard to make but having the pressure of a deadline was even harder.

Elsa had always been against 'taking lives'—that was until she got pregnant herself. The thought of being forced to have a baby against her will became unendurable. As soon as Elsa had come to the conclusion she wouldn't keep the baby (which happened rather quickly), she jumped on the pro-choice bandwagon with delight.

Elsa sat in the waiting room with three other women, each holding a folder. The folders each contained a picture of their baby's fetus. Elsa had asked to not get a picture, but the nurse had included it in her folder anyway. It felt like she had done that on purpose to make sure this is what Elsa wanted. Elsa didn't even look, certain she was making the right choice for herself, the unborn baby, and Simon.

While sitting in the waiting room, Elsa had surreptitiously examined the other three women through sideways glances. They were all very different from her and different from each other. None of them looked very much alike, nor did they share any resembling characteristics. Elsa was not the shortest, not the tallest, or the happiest or most sad. She couldn't relate to any of these women in any way —except one. They had all made the same choice that morning. They had all made the decision to have an abortion.

Elsa was sent home with two large tablets to take; a few hours in between. Twelve hours later she had the worst day of her life. The pain felt like daggers stabbing into her lower back and the ache was like a chainsaw ripping apart her uterus with violence so disturbing it felt like she was starring in a never-ending horror film —where she was stuck in the sequel, the prequel, the remake, and multiple adaptations, even the Broadway musical.

It had been hard for many days after the abortion as well. The physical pain was eventually replaced with guilt and shame, which was almost as bad as the pain of the abortion itself.

Elsa had no idea where these emotions of self-disgust were coming from. Was it biological? Had she already developed motherly feelings for the little dead fetus?

Elsa had never felt real remorse about her decision to have an abortion but she had been very upset about putting herself in the situation, to begin with.

Her decision to have an abortion was the first and only time Elsa had ever prioritized herself.

It's not that she never wanted to have any children, she just didn't want it that particular day.

She felt torn between thinking abortion was wrong and wanting very badly to go through with it.

*

Elsa is grateful that at this moment she doesn't have to explain everything to Gerda in small detail —she seems to understand everything anyway; she is an empath.

"And why haven't you left the person who treats you like shit?"

Along with being an empath, Gerda is also very straightforward and honest, her way of being blunt can be intimidating, especially when she catches you off guard and you get no time to think of a good answer —like normal people would let you do.

Elsa answers, "I guess I am stuck in believing love is stronger than anything."

"How can you be stuck when you have the answer that it isn't working? You're only stuck when you don't have an answer."

"I'm weak."

"You are not weak, you're sensitive, which is the opposite of weakness. Sensitivity is a strength."

*

The next day is Elsa's audition and she's been trembling all afternoon. Gerda has been taking care of her like a mother would take care of a daughter —or like a sister would care for her younger sibling.

Elsa loves how smooth their relationship feels after so little time. Nothing is awkward or embarrassing; even asking for one tampon after another is comfortable. It's soothing and comforting to be nurtured by another woman, and Elsa eats it up.

They lay on the couch, relaxing as they watch 'Together' on the television, a bittersweet comedy about social values and family drama —Gerda's favorite movie.

"This is a very socialist movie," Elsa exclaims thinking it's quite radical.

"It's not really about socialism. On the surface, yes, but it's really about these characters and what they are going through within themselves, and how that reflects on each other."

"Living in a commune is not socialist?" asks Elsa. Gerda just smiles at her.

"You know; I have emotional issues too."

Is this Gerda beginning to actually open up? After all, she hadn't really answered any of Elsa's questions earlier, especially the ones about her age.

"Emotional issues, is that what I have?"

"Sure," says Gerda.

"I'd like to hear about some of yours, now that you have heard about some of mine."

"Maybe."

There's a constant underlying resistance in Gerda. She genuinely wants Elsa around but has built-in limits to how much she can let someone in.

It is Elsa that has opened the pages of her book and read them out loud. Gerda's pages remain closed —her pages are soft and pretty, however, and can still be appreciated without being completely read.

"I know you might not understand my relationship or why I have stayed in it, nobody can understand. Not unless you walk a mile in my shoes, which you can't because they're custom made

—my one foot is a tiny bit bigger than the other— so no one can really understand."

Gerda looks directly into Elsa's eyes.

"I understand," she says.

The Diaries:
ELSA

"Edith Beth Beijer starred in a variety of Scandinavian and European films. She was arguably the biggest Swedish star in the history of cinema. After starring in her first feature film, 'Regnet' (The Rain), she was recognized as a unique actress who was completely natural in style, and without even the need for makeup."

"Film critic Cecilia Fors wrote that she 'Not only bears a startling resemblance to an imaginable human being; she really knows how to act with grace.'"

"FILM ICON EDITH BEIJER DIES AT THE AGE OF THIRTY-SEVEN AFTER CRASHING INTO A TREE IN AN APPARENT SUICIDE WITH HER SIX-YEAR-OLD DAUGHTER IN THE BACKSEAT."

These are only three of the news articles I found cleaning out my mom's storage in Uppsala, where she worked and lived throughout most of her life.

The rumors are true. My mom was a big star; my mom had a borderline personality: and yes, my mom committed suicide. I knew all of this but I had buried it deep down hoping it would never float back up to the surface. Last year it started boiling up in me again and I knew I had to come to terms with my mom's intentions.

Edith had social services after her for many years. They thought of her as an unfit mother and a bad influence for a child.

In the summer of 1998, after years of battling in court with social services, it had been ruled that I, her daughter, was to be taken away from her. Edith's doctor, my nanny, and Edith's agent, all testified against her, all for different reasons.

Mom took her red Volvo 945 with me in the backseat, drove off towards Sodertalje, and crashed the car which caught fire with crazy flames. Flames that I have vivid memories of to this day.

Mom was taken to the hospital but died after seven minutes from organ failure.

I wasn't hurt in the crash, but I was hurt for the rest of my life.

Because nobody knew who my father was, and because I had no other relatives, I was put into the Swedish system. I was thrown into a family consisting of two adults and a child: a couple in their mid-forties, and their seventeen-year-old adopted son.

I was to live there until I turned eighteen, but my time with them was cut short when at the age of twelve I opened up about the truth of what was happening to me in their household.

*

In mom's storage, I found old photos: pictures of her with director Ingmar Bergman, whom she had an affair with as a nineteen-year-old actress studying theatre in Uppsala, which is where they were both from, and where I was born.

Edith was so beautiful —a cross between the actress Greta Garbo and the jazz singer Monica Zetterlund. Lemon blonde hair with cerulean blue eyes, a pointy chin with watermelon colored freckles all over her face. Freckles, just like mine.

There was a long handwritten speech given to Edith from Olof Palme —all I know about him is that he was a Swedish politician, a leader of a new generation of Swedish Social Democrats. I remember that we learned about him in boarding school. Palme was shot dead on an open street in Stockholm in February 1986, while walking home from the cinema with his wife. I was thrilled to learn that my mom was a socialist. Palme was an outspoken supporter of gender equality and women's rights issues.

The speech he had sent my mother was a beautiful feminist speech titled: "The Emancipation of a Man". I wonder why he sent it to her? Because she needed to learn about feminism? Or because she was already a feminist? My mom must have been such a special person, she touched so many hearts with the characters she portrayed in her short life.

"The men should have a larger share in the various aspects of family life, for example, better contact with the children. The women should become economically more independent, get to know fellow-workers and to have contacts with environments outside the home. The greatest gain of increased equality between the sexes would be, of course, that nobody should be forced into a predetermined role on account of sex, but should be given better possibilities to develop his or her personal talents."

The speech goes on for sixteen more pages. I wish he hadn't been murdered, and I wish she hadn't committed suicide so I could talk to them about this speech I had found.

I also found the books my mom used to read to me as a little girl. 'Pelle Svanslos' —various books about a fictional cat living in

Uppsala. Pelle is a kindhearted cat who is constantly bullied by Mans. What I loved about these stories was that all characters in the books were cats, and they were all about good prevailing over evil. I also loved all the movies that were made about Pelle. These human-like cats strutting around the old streets and historical buildings of Uppsala.

Edith's medical records confirmed she was mentally ill, that she had a borderline personality disorder, and that it wasn't getting better with age. By continuing to party, drink, and make movies, all as a way of self-medicating, she had derailed her mental state at a rapid pace.

I used to tackle the thought of inheriting my mom's illness. Although I have never fully accepted the fact she was sick, nor dug into the details of that until now, Edith's illness was too known publicly for me not to be aware of it in the back of my mind. I had heard my foster parents discuss it with teachers at the boarding school I was to be sent to.

The reason I have always suspected I have some kind of disorder is due to the fact I go through mental and physical hell every month, starting ten days prior to menstruating. I know now that I struggle with PMDD —Premenstrual Dysphoric Disorder. I found out about this by going to a clinic in Stockholm. PMS is a walk in the park compared to PMDD. It is a total hijacking of my being where I become a completely different person for ten days.

I started noticing uncomfortable symptoms in my early teens. Everyone would just tell me it was common. I know now that it may be common, but it's not normal.

For me, the ten days leading up to bleeding feel like the earth is shattering beneath me from grief. You can find me sobbing in bed, unable to do anything without having a panic attack or being in a 'light' broken state. The scariest is when I can't really feel anything, which makes me feel like nothing is real, that nothing is really happening, that life isn't happening. I often want to leap in front of a moving car or do something else drastic, like slap myself in the face with no pause just to see if I will feel it or not. Avoiding the world is something I've come to terms with that I need to do every month.

When I was fifteen years old I started seeing a female healthcare professional. I told her about the symptoms I was having.

"I can't make a decision," I told her.

"You can't make a decision?"

"I act out of rage and impulse, I scream into a pillow. I feel like the whole world is going under."

"You feel like the whole world is going under?"

After repeating all my answers as questions she prescribed me birth control guarantying it would help control my emotions.

The pill worked for a few years so I kept on taking them, especially after my abortion. I was glad it had an effect to a certain degree but a year ago the effect started to wear off. Then it seemed to do more harm than good. Sure, it helped eliminate some of the cramping, but I started feeling even more depressed without knowing why.

I've learned today (after years of being a slave to the pill), that the pill shuts down ovulation, and that women *need* to ovulate. A woman has the right to do whatever she wants with her body, but we need to be informed about how our body alerts us, which I was not. It turned out the pill was merely masking my underlying hormonal imbalance, especially my emotional imbalance. Traumatic experiences such as suppressing the fact Edith's intention was to kill us both in the car crash that day, meaning my own mom wanted me dead had their effect. Why did my own mom want to end my life? How could she be so selfish? What had I done to deserve being killed? Why did she bring me into this world only to try and take me out of it?

This past year I've tried therapy to help me understand my mom's illness. I have big questions that I am still trying to get answers to. I feel a huge sense of abandonment from both my mom and dad (whom I still don't know a single thing about).

I wish I knew who my parents really were. Not just the woman on screen or the man in my fantasies, but really knew who they were. I want to know if my dad loved my mom. Did he know he had a daughter somewhere? My foster parents told me I was probably made on a drunken night with a complete stranger — unfortunately, I think that is probably true.

The trauma I went through during the years of staying with my foster parents is still not completely healed, but I am getting help.

I promise myself I will never get on the pill again. I never knew that being on birth control could come with so many side effects, no one informed me. It robbed me of several years of my life, making me miserable. I will never let a stranger come into my body and mess with my digestive system and cause my vagina to dry up ever again. But getting hormonal birth control was the only way to get off this vicious cycle of despair. Today I have found a more holistic approach to my PMDD —it hasn't gone away, and probably never will completely, but it has gotten better.

The more I heal the wounds from my traumatic past, the more I am in balance with my menstruation. I think everything is connected to everything.

My anxiety prior to bleeding is connected to something inside of me that tells me something is wrong. That feeling was masked in emotions; cramps and sadness became louder and louder each year and every month until I couldn't ignore the symptoms anymore. The pill helped mask it for a few years, but then it all got worse as I've said.

Living in misalignment with my values resulted in anxiety for years —it was at its height during my years at boarding school.

I felt abandoned and shameful of what had happened to me during the time with my foster parents. I felt dirty and disgusting and instead of addressing the underlying factors, I covered it up by never diving into my past.

*

My first time bleeding was when I was around twelve years old, and it was caused by my foster brother raping me which broke my hymen. I didn't tell anyone about it for two years. My 'real' menstrual cycle started when I was fourteen and living at the boarding school.

When I told my foster parents about what had happened they immediately sent me to boarding school. I was happy I didn't have to live under the same roof as him anymore.

The day I started bleeding, my period came out of nowhere with no warning. Leaving ballet class, I felt unusual cramps in my lower stomach. I went to the bathroom and saw pink/brownish spots on the toilet paper after wiping. I hated the feeling -- it threw me right into those horrible nights with my foster brother creeping around my bedroom as he waited for my foster parents to go to sleep so he could abuse me.

The beginning of my 'real' period marks the day I began to connect my menstruation to having been raped.

I strongly believe that my suffering during my period was connected to that memory of mine. My body went into a PTSD mode, connecting my monthly bleeding to those 'horrible nights'. My periods made me feel shameful, reminding me of what had happened on those nights. Month after month, it was a reminder of how dirty I was.

My periods began to come unexpectedly and even more brutally with each passing month. On the first day of bleeding, I'd beg the teachers to let me stay in bed. They didn't at first.

"All women go through menstruation, you're not a special case," they'd say.

They changed their minds when they'd come to get me and I'd vomit all over them because the cramps were so bad.

The depression would manifest in multiple ways on top of my overall social anxiety, and I got Swedish seasonal depression from hell.

My period was never looked upon as an illness but today I know different. No one could understand what I was going through.

My two roommates and I were always synced and menstruating at the same time. That was the only connection I ever felt with them. Although I hated them, I felt close to them during that time of the month. I felt less lonely in it but I hated them because their symptoms were things like: 'in the mood for chocolate'. They were 'irritable', while my symptoms were 'trying not to jump in front of a train'.

I did not appreciate my relationship with them because it felt like they were always trying to drain me. All the girls I met at boarding school were pleasantly cut out of my life after graduation. I couldn't handle it anymore. I couldn't handle being their emotional support when I was barely brave enough to look into my own shit. These girls seemed to think that friendship was all about pouring their negative toxic energy down your throat. The only time they'd want to have 'quality time' was when they had something to bitch about. That was never what friendship meant to me. Friendship to me is checking in, following up with somebody, asking about how that thing they were thinking of doing is coming along, about how they are feeling, and really show up. I never got that from those girls.

The struggle for self-worth was unbearable during boarding school. I had no one to talk to. The other girls knew my periods were rough, but no one ever asked if there was something they could do for me —they'd just stay away. No one even offered me ibuprofen, like it would make their daddies stocks go down if they did. Selfish rich people.

I feel empathy for the teenage me. The teenager who felt so alone and shamed by the fact she would bleed through a super plus tampon in an hour. The teenager who wished so hard for a safe place to figure this whole bleeding thing out. I know she felt lonely stumbling through something she knew so little about. I bled through so many times, in the worst of situations, each time making me feel more like there was something wrong with me because I couldn't handle the most intuitive of womanly things.

I think menstruating sucks but it's a part of life and something we all need to accept; men and women. It's not talked about enough and that makes me sad. It's seen as a 'gross' thing that happens to women, but it's so much more than that.

We are powerful beings who lead reproduction and that makes women magical —so bleeding is the last thing I am going to feel embarrassed about. It's up to me as a woman to take the lead and feel proud of my body and all its processes and functions. Being cyclical makes us connected to nature, especially the moon. Can't you feel the change emotionally when the moon changes face? I've come to feel that bleeding is something mystical. I'm sure it is a gift of nature. We can't expect men to feel comfortable with women's bleeding if we ourselves are constantly hiding it and feeling ashamed.

My worst period happened when I was volunteering in the kitchen at my boarding school at the age of fifteen. I was chopping onions (like that wasn't hard enough) when suddenly I felt I had bled through my super-plus tampon. I had to finish my shift before going back to my dorm because the male manager of the kitchen wouldn't let me go until the work was done. I was humiliated —everyone knew what was going on— and it left a stain on the wood floor. A stain that would haunt me for a long time after that. It was sad and embarrassing and no one felt any compassion for me.

"You should've been prepared!" as the male manager expressed it.

My name is Elsa Vera Beijer, I am one of those people on earth —a woman— who dictates the progression of the human race and for that, and I'd like some fucking respect. I'm not fishing…Well maybe just a little.

*

Today I understand that I couldn't talk to anyone about this because it meant I'd have to tell them the truth about the horrible nights. The reason I understand this today is because now I know that everything is connected to everything. I had to know that my menstrual symptoms and all the associated trauma were connected to the horrible nights. Why else would I never open up to anyone? My womanly intuition and all my emotions must have connected those dots, while my intellect avoided it at all costs.

In my last year at the boarding school, I started to see a therapist (I wish I'd started seeing her much sooner). She was a young and vibrant woman in her thirties, Eva, and she was absolutely incredible in her approach. She was the only person except for my foster parents, who I ever opened up to about the horrible nights.

Eva made me tell her everything. But I still refused to talk about Edith. That wasn't going to happen until now.

Eva told me something that even though I haven't always applied it, it has always stuck with me:

"To live well is the best revenge."

She said people always have two choices when facing trauma. Number one: *Fuck everything and run*. Or number two: *Face everything and recover*. For years I chose number one and stayed in an abusive relationship. I never faced my inner demons, until now.

I now fully comprehend why I stayed with Voldemort. I've never been a traditional person, yet I dreamed of having a wedding. Why is it so ingrained in us women to want that no matter how evolved, independent, and non-traditional we are? I don't have that answer yet, but I will for sure spend the rest of my life trying to figure it out.

From now on I will also strongly choose number two: *Face everything and recover*. There is no point in letting anything else control my life —especially my past. All I can do now is live my best life and leave everything else behind. It's a simple concept and sometimes a bit corny, but so true.

Edith will never be left behind again. Digging into her history is something I will continue to do forever; she is part of me and I want to understand her disease. I want to understand why she suffered so much, and what she found happiness in.

For many years I resented Edith. I hated her for not being there to protect me. I no longer think it was her responsibility to save me because now I understand she couldn't even save herself. And that's not Edith's fault. That's not mom's fault. *My* mom's fault.

Burnt Offerings

I t is one hour until Birgit's funeral, and fifty minutes until Elsa's audition. Marie closes the front door to the bakery and locks up from the inside, she needs to fill two quick orders before she can walk over to the church where the funeral is being held. Marie can't remember the last time she felt so alone. With Elsa at her audition and Amira still being in London she will be attending the funeral on her own. A few of Birgit's old friends will be there but no family members as far as she knows.

*

Gerda drops Elsa off at her audition —they give each other a big warm hug with no words. The best kind of hug.

"I'll pick you up afterward if you want?" offers Gerda after being released from the embrace.

"I think I feel like walking, but I'll call you later."

The number of people auditioning since last time seems to have tripled. Or is this perception just from her nerves? She is doing a monologue from August Strindberg's "Miss Julie" and is feeling more confident than last time. She starts to stretch. People's looks in her direction are not bothering her today.

A woman with curly black hair moves close to Elsa and rolls her yoga mat out right next to her.

"Are you Edith Beijer's daughter?" the woman asks.

*

There are seven other people in the church. All spread out in the pews not talking to each other. There is a black and white photo of a smiling Birgit on a tripod next to the linen white coffin that has twin flowers sitting on top of it.

*

"Elsa Vera Beijer. We are ready for you."

*

Nothing can prepare you to lose a mother. Marie knows that the only link she had to her sister was their mother. That link is now dead or changed, depending on whatever happens after someone dies. Definitely changed.

Marie thinks back on how she used to talk back to Birgit, how she used to roll her eyes at her mother then mutter and walk away. Would it have been easier if Birgit had died young? Would it have been easier to grieve because the memories would have been less? Birgit had been very controlling and manipulative at times, but Marie learned to love her mother for who she was. She had worked hard to forgive and understand her.

Today Marie feels like her heart has been taken hostage, her mind like a broken record repeating events. Mostly their fights. Guilt is what shows up the most.

She fears she'll never get over this. Does the pain of losing a mother ever really go away? The big questions are unbearable. They say time heals everything, but for Marie, this moment will never heal —maybe it will shift and change, transform, go up and down, but it will stay.

Everyone has a moment where their life *really* changes. This is Marie's moment.

Her mother is forever gone. She will never see her again. She will never again feel her mother's skin moisturized with unscented Nivea lotion, never see her in person again. But in Marie's memory, Birgit is only one second away. That thought comforts her while she bends down her head, letting the rapid tears march like aggressive soldiers down her cheeks.

The thought flashes through her that death seems somewhat poetic —dark, as poetry can sometimes be. How many lives has Birgit touched? Questions keep coming through her tears. Probably not many, Birgit had been very alone for the last twenty years of her life. But had Birgit ever inspired anyone? She was after all a teacher of junior high students once upon a time. Maybe Birgit is the reason for someone's happiness today? Maybe she helped someone out of an addiction? Perhaps she told someone to follow their dreams. Maybe she was that kind of influence to everyone but her own daughters.

Marie sits there sobbing in what she feels is the deepest and most tragic moment of her life. A hand touches her shoulder from behind —she turns around to see Elsa sitting in the back aisle smiling with a smile as big and warm as a smile can get.

"Little swan, what are you doing here?" Marie asks, surprised.

She looks at her watch and it tells her Elsa is fifteen minutes late to her audition.

"You should get going! You should be there by now!"

"I'm not doing it. I decided to be here with you instead."

"What are you talking about?"

Marie feels a pang of immense guilt. Elsa is skipping this important audition to be here with her.

"You shouldn't miss the audition for this!"

"I thought you would be in need of a friend."

Elsa jumps over the pew to sit next to Marie who finds this very touching. For the first time Marie decides to just give in and receive her friend's kindness. She won't say no or argue against it anymore.

For the first time it feels like someone has chosen her —put her in the first place, and that person is Elsa. She is to do nothing but receive from her young friend. Elsa grabs Marie's left hand and strokes her scar with her ice cold fingers.

The Diaries:
MARIE

Parents can do a lot of damage to their children. I am not a parent myself but logic comes in handy. When it comes to raising a child it's easy to make mistakes. I've both heard about it and seen it up close.

In April 1959, when Cilla and I were just eight months old a fire ruined our home, family, and some of our skin —mostly Cilla's. We were sleeping close together in our shared crib. Our parents were woken up by the smell of smoke from our bedroom, which was next to theirs. My father was choking on the smoke and told my mother to get us girls and run outside, so she braved the fire in our room, grabbed us into her arms, and climbed out the window to save us, which she did.

Cilla was the most severely injured, suffering third-degree burns on twenty percent of her body. Her whole chest, stomach, and right leg were badly burned. There were visible welts on her right cheek all the way down to the neck. Only my left hand and parts of my left chin were injured.

Firefighters rescued my father who had struggled because of the heavy smoke. They found him unconscious and he died three days later as a result of smoke inhalation.

Cilla and I have no memory of the fire nor of our father whose name was Bengt. We don't recall any of our life before that event. Cilla had to do years of therapy to regain full use of her hands and her right leg.

When Cilla and I turned seven years old our mother Birgit talked to us about the fire for the first time. She told us how our father had died while assuring we would get out safely before him. It makes me angry that he didn't run to our bedroom and climb out of the window as well. Our father would have been alive today had he done that; I guess it's hard to think when one is in a panic.

Birgit wasn't hurt by the fire physically, but she was damaged in all kinds of other ways. She was left afraid of fire for the rest of her life. She would beat me and my sister if we ever played with fire. One time she beat us so badly I thought she had lost her mind for a few moments —all because we had lit a candle when she wasn't home. Her way of loving was to sometimes physically abuse us from time to time.

Cilla grew more and more conscious of her appearance as we grew older and was being teased by children in our preschool. Our mother told Cilla that she was unique and that her scars were a sign of bravery, but that didn't help. At the age of nine, Cilla was seeing a psychologist who reported she was suffering from depression. We were so close back then. Our old teachers say they never saw us separately on any occasion and that we were always holding hands. Cilla never wanted to wear t-shirts and preferred shawls all year round, but nothing would cover her right cheek, neck, and both her hands.

High school was cruel and she had to endure being bullied almost every day. I would beat up the bullies in our class, I'd even try to ignore them, but nothing would make them back down.

We were only fifteen when I noticed Cilla was sinking into a darker and darker hole.

Birgit and I both felt helpless. There was nothing we could say or do to make her feel better about herself. At least the physical beatings stopped by that time.

My mother felt a tremendous amount of guilt which resulted in guilty parenting, not a good thing. Cilla started to smoke and drink but my mother just turned the other cheek. She tried to talk sense to my sister but Cilla would only talk back —or rather scream back.

"You ruined my life!" she'd yell at our mother.

We eventually found out that the house burned down because my mother had left two candles lit next to our curtains.

Out of guilt, my mom would constantly try to please Cilla. I felt like I was being cast aside so that Cilla would feel good.

*

Around seventeen, Cilla's hate and rage towards her appearance was directed onto me the most.

Although we were identical and beautiful twins, the one difference was that of Cilla's scars.

She started throwing fits around the house every chance she could get. I remember she cut the television cable off once just to spite my mother. How did my mother respond? —By not responding much. She would just turn to me afterward and say:

"Be nice to your sister, she's gone through a lot."

Like I wasn't going through a lot with everything that was going on? I didn't have the same amount of scars but I was also in that fire, I lost my father too!

My mother overcompensated for her guilt towards Cilla with an unhealthy lack of discipline. Cilla was never held accountable for her cruel actions or the physical violence she exhibited in our home.

My greatest sorrow in life was seeing my sister's pain every day. Although every time I had the slightest issue or emotional problem she would be quick to attack me:

"Well, I live with ugly burn scars and you don't!"

Cilla was tough towards my mother and me at home, but quiet and timid like a mouse in school.

On our eighteen birthday, February 6th, she stole my mother's car and crashed it. When she got back home my mother refused to be hard on her:

"It's okay Cilla, you didn't mean to do it."

Cilla kept getting away with horrid behavior and was given all the freedom in the world.

Mother would parent from her guilt rather than doing what was best or right for my sister.

It felt as if mother would almost reward her poor behavior. When I'd speak up about this my mother would defend her by making up excuses.

She wanted Cilla to have all the choices in the world. She'd let Cilla abuse her verbally and emotionally, and Cilla would further terrorize her with extreme picky eating. She'd even tell mother to get out of her face whenever she didn't feel like engaging.

My mother's health started declining —she lost twenty pounds— her job due to depression and could no longer leave the house. I had to get a job as a cashier at a grocery store. We couldn't make it financially with me working only a few shifts so I had to quit college at the age of twenty-three so I could help my mother with rent and all other bills.

Cilla wasn't doing anything at that time; she'd lay home and watch television all day, recovering from hangovers. It's not that Cilla would drink with friends —she didn't have any. She'd drink alone sitting in parks.

Mother kept giving Cilla anything she wanted anytime she wanted it. She would never argue back with Cilla. It was now the guilt mixed with my mother's own depression.

Cilla smoked cigarettes inside with no one commenting on it —If I'd go against Cilla, mother would just defend her so I stopped. She'd put her dirty shoes up on the table (without looks from anyone), and play loud and horrible hard rock music (with no excuse).

Cilla became horrible to be around. One of the worst things she ever did to my mom was to spit her straight in the face with no provocation. And the worst thing she ever did to me was to ruin a date I had been looking forward to for weeks.

*

His name was Hampus. I was twenty-four and still working at the grocery store. I had dated a guy earlier that previous year who gave me genital herpes. Both mother and Cilla knew about it. We knew everything about each other. Mother had found my Valtrex (medicine for an outbreak), and I told them I had discovered sores on my vagina that proved to be herpes.

Cilla hugged me for the second time in our lives and said she felt sorry. Mother tried to pretend she didn't understand anything about this but I know she did.

When Hampus and I started flirting, it had only been six months since I'd been diagnosed. I felt shame, guilt (which seems to run in my family), and had no idea how or when to tell him about my condition.

Hampus arrived at our doorstep to pick me up for our second date. The first one had been lovely; we had taken a walk on Kungsholmen in Stockholm and talked until about four in the morning.

On the second date, we planned to go see a movie and I was still preparing when he showed up. Cilla answered the door. I told them I'd be right down.

When I got downstairs Hampus was gone, Cilla was drunk and laughing. Mother was in her bedroom sleeping (what she spent most of her time doing).

"Where is he? Did he leave?"

"Of course he did, when I told him the truth about you."

"What do you mean?"

"That you're an infected slut."

I felt my body vibrate into a million pieces and dissolve into the air. I understood she had told Hampus about my herpes. The biggest betrayal in my life came from my own sister.

"He deserves to know. You can't go around fucking people with a bunch of viruses."

I couldn't believe it. I always understood that Cilla carried a lot of pain and sorrow in her heart because of her scars, but did she really carry this much hatred?

The tears fell down on my cheek, not streaming but rather in slow motion and similar to a romantic comedy. Time stood still.

"I will never forgive you for this."

"Have I asked for your forgiveness herpie?"

I don't think I have ever forgiven her for telling Hampus what she did. The hug she gave me the day she found out what the Valtrex tablets were for was not out of love —that hug came from the fact she was happy that I wasn't the 'perfect one' anymore.

I don't know what hurt the most. The fact that my own sister had betrayed me or the fact that my own sister was in so much pain.

It's not that I wasn't going to tell Hampus before we did anything, it's just that I wanted to tell him myself, in my own way. I had decided what I was going to say and how I was going to say it.

My doctor had said it would be better to say:

"I carry the herpes virus,"

Rather than:

"I have herpes,"

That's what I was going to tell him, but Cilla didn't allow that to happen.

Cilla ruined my 'acceptance of the virus journey' —she had made it a thousand times worse.

It would be seven years until I dated anyone again.

For years I carried feelings of guilt, shame, and hate towards myself and my own body. I felt like I had done something to deserve getting this virus.

Cilla had been burned and damaged so of course, I had to suffer one way or the other.

Cilla eventually moved out with a guy and it would be two years until we heard a word from her again.

By then our grandmother who I had known very little of died and left us all "The Swedish Bakery". With my mother's depression and Cilla's disappearance, I had to take it over at the age of thirty-one. I was still working at the grocery store so it felt like a gift when it came to me. I'd always wanted to teach yoga in a warmer climate and figured that working in a bakery for a while would help with the expenses.

Mother checked into a mental hospital to get help and I rented an apartment in the city so I could be close to the bakery. I learned everything I had to in order to run it —little did I know I was to stay here for more than twenty-five years.

Cilla was the only thing my mother asked about every time I visited her at the institution. Not once did she ask how I was doing, how the bakery was coming along, or what I wanted out of life.

"Still haven't heard anything from your sister?" she'd ask worryingly and repetitively.

I think the major problem with Cilla was that she was given too much freedom because now she's sixty (like me), and suffering from way too much freedom. She can swim wherever she wants in life, do whatever she wants, float everywhere with no shore to swim back to. For her whole life, she could say and do exactly what she wanted without any boundaries or guidelines.

How is that supposed to help you in life? How can a person learn when nobody tells them what not to do?

How are you supposed to understand you're doing something unhealthy for yourself when you're not experiencing any consequences?

I call it toxic parenting because one day it will be impossible for the child to know what it wants because he or she hasn't been given limits.

*

When it comes to my herpes. I forgive myself. I did a long time ago. It is not as disgusting as we make it in our minds. It's still taboo in polite society, but who cares?

My best advice to everyone is to get over it. It's just a virus that causes a skin condition every now and then. Relax, don't eat too much sugar, have your vitamins handy, and take Valtrex when you feel an outbreak coming. That's it.

I forgive myself for those seven years of terror I caused myself. It wasn't my fault and I am not less worthy of love because of a virus I contracted.

I forgive myself for constantly trying to be perfect believing it would make my mother happy and cure her depression. I believed my actions had a large impact on my mother's emotions and well-being. They didn't.

I forgive myself for running away from my problems and never facing them eye to eye, for pretending I have a fabulous life on social media (everyone does that though, so I don't feel that guilty, to begin with).

My mother's guilt was never a helpful emotion. The guilt made all family issues become about my mother. Guilt is not about the other person, the child (in this case Cilla), but comes from the parent's failures. Parents make mistakes, children get mad, and that's all there is to it. All this tip-toeing around and kissing children's asses only turns them into shitty people. Witnessing this with my sister, I've learned that parenting is a lot about learning to forgive yourself for your own mistakes.

My biggest hope is that my mother before slipping into dementia, had one minute if only one minute to forgive herself for all her well-intentioned parenting that went wrong. My dear mother wore Cilla as a badge on her chest and blamed herself for all of Cilla's failures.

Parents should know that they can't claim their child's failures or successes as their own because frankly, they have little to do with either one. Everyone chooses who they are or want to be and at a certain point, it is not the parent's responsibility anymore. Every bird leaves its nest.

I forgive my mother for not letting me be heard and constantly choosing my sister's emotions over mine. Parents are not superheroes and we have to stop expecting them to be. Mother did the best she could, the best she understood, and the best she knew.

I forgive you too, Cilla. I don't know exactly why but I feel it's time to let go of my anger at you. For myself more than for you. I'm sorry I didn't get as much burn damage as you and I am sorry I couldn't find a way to take your pain away. I understand now that drinking isn't an egotistical action but a terrible disease. I am sorry I haven't been able to comprehend that until now.

I don't know why I was assigned Cilla and mother in this lifetime. Perhaps I had karmic things to solve. What I do know is that it is important to cut emotional and energetic bonds with family members. The ties that bind. This doesn't mean that you have to cut the love you feel for them, it just means you're protecting yourself from something that isn't feeding your soul. The problem with me is I never did cut those bonds with my family and that has caused immense sadness in my life. But it's okay because now I do cut them. I will no longer suffer from the things of the past that I can't control or change, and I no longer hold myself accountable for other people's miseries and sorrows. For that, I also forgive myself.

The idyllic Carl Larsson paintings that had for so long awakened emotions of bliss and happiness in my imagination finally arrived as a truth in my life, not in the traditional way as seen in the paintings —house, husband, and children— but as the *feelings* of those things. The painting of my life turned out differently than a generic version of contentment. I painted it on my own, and in some ways, it was easier than I had thought —I stopped pushing for the perfect picture, and instead, I dived into the flow of life without resistance.

In the same way, I'd get used to a laundry machine, I stopped obsessing about cycle options, stopped smelling the drum for left behind bleach, and I quit overpacking the machine with whatever would fit. Just like that Elsa, my little swan slid into my life and added just the right amount of fabric softener, or how Amira, my other little swan, inserted the proper number of coins into the slot. They pressed the 'Start' button for me.

Life is not a rational linear stream of events and happenings, it is a rollercoaster full of surprises. Tragedy and healing. For some people, life *really* starts later in the ride. I feel like I am flourishing more than ever before. I forgive myself for not forgiving myself until now.

Seven Types of Cake

The few moments where Swedish women could connect and meet without men and children being present during the beginning of the nineteenth century was when a Fika was flung together by the women of the villages. It became a tradition to make seven types of cakes, preferably including some sort of wheat loaf, sponge cakes, both light and dark, biscuits, and pastries.

These Fika affairs were more easy-going than the big parties or dinners that were usually held at that time. You'd be better off if you were disciplined with the number of cakes served at the gatherings. If you served more than seven cakes you'd be looked upon as bumptious, and if you served less than seven you'd be regarded as cheap. Seven cakes were considered to be 'lagom' (moderate and good enough).

In jubilant celebration of this tradition Elsa and Marie bake seven types of cakes every year on June twenty-fourth, marking and celebrating Midsummer Eve together with Amira before driving out to Marie's summer house on an island of the

Stockholm Archipelago. Once Elsa had split from Voldemort Amira was back in her life closer than ever before.

This is the fourth time these women of the bakery have engaged in this ingrained ritual together, only this time they are joined by Gerda and her strange rabbit Lotta.

That morning Marie had a sweet phone call with her sister Cilla who is in rehab and recovering slowly. Birgit's death seemed to have awakened something in Cilla, including her connection to Marie.

Elsa has hung a picture of Maries's late mother on the wall behind the bakery counter. Five females are there in the bakery for the occasion. Marie, Elsa, Amira, Gerda, and Lotta. Counting Cilla and Edith in spirit, there are seven. One kind of cake for each of them (including the rabbit).

In a woven basket, Elsa carries the seven types of cakes: *limpa* (Swedish rye bread), a light and airy sponge cake topped with blueberries and whip cream, a black forest gateau with a side of cherries, *havreflarn* (Swedish oat crisps), oatmeal cookies that are sandwiched together with chocolate milk, *Dammsugare* (The Swedish word for vacuum cleaner) because vacuum cleaners there used to have the same colors as these green and brown marzipan punsch-rolls, and finally vanilla hearts —a love heart-shaped pastry dusted with vanilla sugar.

The seven of them (two in spirit) drive to the ferry that will take them to the island where Marie's summer house abides, each of them abandoning their homes so that they can escape the city to retire in front of the water, enjoying each other's company for five whole days.

Like many cottages, houses, and barns in Sweden, Marie's summer house is painted with red paint that comes from the copper mines. The paint is made by the blending of rye flour, linseed oil, tailings from the Swedish copper mines, and water. The Dala horse red paint goes well with the white trim.

The women stand in front of the cottage for a moment with a sense of accomplishment at having arrived, then jubilation upon entering.

They've decided to do nothing but flee their everyday obligations, dwell in their friendship, hear about the further development of Amira's career as a journalist, appreciate their uniqueness, and let Lotta jump around and binge on pastries.

Overbaked

They have been in this place where time doesn't exist for two whole days. Having barbecues, braiding each other's hair, and mostly playing Kubb (a lawn game) knocking over each other's wooden blocks with confidence. Marie and Elsa against Gerda and Amira; Amira and Elsa against Marie and Gerda.

In the evenings they take turns choosing a movie. Tonight they are watching Lasse Hallstrom's "My Life As a Dog" — Gerda is scratching Marie's back because Marie has been having trouble sleeping ever since they got here. Gerda has been kind enough to show her some extra care, and this evening gave Marie one of her sleeping pills, but it hasn't kicked in yet. Marie gets up to do the dishes before taking a much-needed bath leaving the others to bond without her dampening presence.

While pouring the water into the bathtub Marie debates with her herself whether she should wash her hair tonight or not. She slides into the bathtub with water still running, adding Epsom salt and three drops of lavender oil.

Since she won't be swimming in the lake tomorrow (it's going to be a rainy day) Marie decides to wash her hair and get it over with for the next couple of days. She sniffs the lavender scent with delight as she leans her head forward and starts to wash her hair, feeling so relaxed and happy at hearing the young women's laughter drift up from downstairs.

Marie plays her favorite song on her phone as she languidly washes away:

Skeeter Davis — "A Summer Place".

She has only the conditioning left to do.

*

Amira shows Elsa and Gerda a few magic tricks with a card deck that she learned from a YouTube video —neither of them is particularly impressed.

The fireplace is crackling with a soft touch.

"What are we going to do tomorrow? It's going to rain all fucking day," Elsa says disappointed, given she had planned to swim every day.

"You can swim anyway, no one is stopping you," Amira retorts.

A relaxing time at a cottage out in the blue hasn't made Amira's attitude any less harsh.

"I'm going to go check in on Marie," Gerda tells them as she leaves the quarreling besties behind and goes upstairs.

"Tell her to turn the sound of the music down," Amira calls out.

Elsa agrees and joins in:

"Tell Marie to stop playing that song on repeat, we're going deaf here."

*

Gerda stands in the doorway of the bathroom. It's as if the whole world has stopped, the bittersweet melody of the song is the only thing she can hear. It fills the space until only the individual notes remain. Skeeter Davis's singing voice carries on. She stands paralyzed, staring at the backside of Marie's head floating face down in the shallow bathwater. Marie's blonde greyish hair swirls from one side to the other like the slow-motion tentacles of an octopus. Her hair seems peaceful as if guided by the peaceful rhythms of 'A Summer Place'.

She must have done something —screamed, moved, something— but Gerda's only memory is of people running up and down the stairs; an ambulance siren going loud as a bomb. But yet she still stood paralyzed, watching the dancing octopus that was no longer there.

The fire alarm went off, the smell of burnt bread filled the idyllic cottage in the Swedish countryside.

*

June fourteenth would be the last Instagram post Marie ever made: a picture of herself, Elsa, Amira, and Gerda holding her rabbit, all in the bright sun on the ferry's deck as they made their way to the island. That post would have more comments and likes than any of her previous ones: "Rest in Peace" — "Can't believe this tragedy"— "The bakery will never shine as bright without you". And: "What happened to Marie? Does anyone know?"

*

A sign hangs on the door:

"THE SWEDISH BAKERY WILL REMAIN CLOSED UNTIL FURTHER NOTICE."

Made in the USA
Monee, IL
24 August 2022

12337534R00100